Death of a Man-Tamer

Paul Phelan, who was once a [...] now traps rare wild animal[s...] believes he is a conservationi[st...] captured, stripped naked, and [...] be taught what it is like to be a[...]

His captors are women wh[o...] animal rights group and their leader is someone skilled in training men to obey commands.

Once free Phelan is determined to exact revenge on his captors, at whatever peril to himself, but first he must find them. To this end he employs a private detective, John Samson. But, in the meantime, and unknown to both, the hunter has become the hunted, and Phelan is in danger of losing his liberty permanently.

John Samson, the fat detective who is privately obsessed with the concept of Time, has featured in several of Miles Tripp's novels. And Paul Phelan has appeared before as the main character in the brilliant *The Skin Dealer*. They combine here to resolve a very powerful plot played out against a fascinating background of fringe animal rights campaigners and prostitutes who specialise in male domination.

Miles Tripp, always a writer whose talent takes a special and original form, is at the height of his powers in this absorbing new crime novel.

Miles Tripp

DEATH OF A MAN-TAMER

PENZ

MACMILLAN
LONDON

First published 1987 by
MACMILLAN LONDON LIMITED
4 Little Essex Street London WC2R 3LF
and Basingstoke

Associated companies in Auckland, Delhi, Dublin, Gaborone, Hamburg, Harare, Hong Kong, Johannesburg, Kuala Lumpur, Lagos, Manzini, Melbourne, Mexico City, Nairobi, New York, Singapore and Tokyo

British Library Cataloguing in Publication Data

Tripp, Miles
    Death of a man-tamer.
    I. Title
    823′.914[F]   PR6070.R48
    ISBN 0-333-40742-3

Typeset in Bembo by Bookworm Typesetting, Manchester

Printed and bound in Great Britain by Anchor Brendon Ltd, Essex

CHAPTER 1

He was driving a car across a salt-pan towards a herd of zebras. Dust stirred by their hooves formed a pale, hovering mist over the surface of the pan and, above this mist, striped bodies stood in sharp relief against an electric blue sky. As he drew closer to the herd some zebras skittered nervously; it was as though an alarm signal was zigzagging through the black and white maze of twisting bodies.

He put his foot on the brake, but the car accelerated before it suddenly vaporised around him and now he was lying on his back on a hard crust of salt with a zebra rearing above, its hooves pawing the air. He tried to hurl himself to one side and as he did so the zebra stripes became the bars of a cage. The dream faded as he surfaced into consciousness.

Reality was more disconcerting than the dream. He was in a cage and the cage was in a room without windows. He had no idea why he was here or how he had come to be here. Because life in the wild had taught him that to remain horizontal was to be vulnerable he staggered to his feet. As he stood up he realised with a shock that he was naked. Even the watch had been taken from his wrist. For a moment he gazed with disbelief at the pelt of hair on his chest and the mat of hair below his belly. Who had stripped him and why?

He had enemies. All men who lived full lives had enemies. You could philosophise about civilisation and morality but basically men were tribal beings who fought other tribes when they weren't fighting each other. You couldn't wipe out millions of years of prehistory by a few thousand years of agriculture and a few hundred years of industrial effort, or by Beethoven or Rembrandt. Men were natural enemies of each other, but which enemy had put him in a cage and taken away his clothes?

5

He remembered leaving a television studio to look for a taxi. He had been jostled in the street and felt something sharp pierce his arm. He looked down and saw a small reddish patch against sun-tanned skin. Someone must have injected him with a drug before bundling him into a getaway car. It had been a skilled operation on a busy London street.

Milos was an enemy. In a bar of the Connaught Hotel in Madras, Milos had sworn to get him one day. He had sabotaged an ivory deal which Milos had set up, but if you loved elephants, Indian or African, you didn't play fair with men like Milos, and to get the better of a Greek in a financial deal was inviting enmity. The Madras connection might be the clue. Who else? It was easier to list enemies than friends. Friends who could be trusted were very few. Murunga, warehouse foreman and gun-bearer, had once saved his life and could be trusted but Murunga was thousands of miles away.

He looked around. A flight of stairs ran down one side of the room which was illuminated by three neon strips. A cavity at the top of the stairs seemed to be a ventilation shaft. The floor was covered by square brown lino-tiles and an electric fire was plugged into a socket on one wall. But it was the other walls which arrested his attention. Hanging on hooks were manacles, leather harnesses, dog collars and leads, an assortment of whips and canes and a strait-jacket. Apart from these mural fittings the only other piece of furniture in the room was an oblong wooden frame, slightly raised above the floor, which had bars with winding mechanisms at each end. He had never seen such a contraption before but guessed it was a rack.

He was obviously in a cellar or basement which had once been used as a torture chamber, but at least he wasn't shackled and could move freely round the cage which contained a mattress and an Elsan. Having assimilated his environment he looked for some means of escape. The cage bars were well spaced but not wide enough to allow him to squeeze through. A barred door was secured by chain and padlock. He pulled at the padlock hasp and shook the chain so that it rattled noisily but his efforts were futile.

Proud men don't shout for help and he was proud. He prowled round the confines of the cage like a trapped tiger and thought of men who hated him enough to kidnap and cage him like a wild animal. Apart from Milos and some other traders there had been one or two men who had resented their womenfolk being attracted to him. One man in particular, an Armenian merchant married to a French woman, had sworn to kill him one day.

Momentarily he paused from pacing and tried to remember the man's name. Like nearly all Armenian names it must have ended in 'ian' but he couldn't recall it. In recent years it had become increasingly difficult to remember names of people although strangely he could recollect the name of every cat and dog he had ever owned and the names he'd given to some wild animals. He gave up trying to recall the man's name but remembered his wife was called Solange. He hadn't encouraged her but she'd turned up at his house one night and they'd both had too much to drink.

Solange had pierced nipples and a fish tattooed on the inside of her left thigh. The fish resembled a gurnard with heavy head and finger-like pectoral fins but she had called it an *hirondelle de mer*. 'In English, a swallow fish,' she had said and had accompanied the translation with a coarse, meaning laugh.

The memory of Solange and her husband faded and he continued pacing an area measuring three by three metres.

There were many men he could count as enemies but none who would trap him in a cowardly fashion with a concealed hypodermic syringe. But enemies weren't always men who put their money or their self-esteem on the line, they could be hostile unknowns like the television chat-show presenter. She had been unknown to him although she might have been known to the millions of passive no-hopers who watched television night after night.

The presenter had needled him. From the moment they were introduced before the show he knew that she was an adversary. She'd given him a disdainful look and said, 'It makes it better if we don't rehearse what we're going to talk about but I'll let you know it'll be about the white tigers.'

'What else?' he had replied. 'That's what makes me news. The fact that I'm dedicated to conservation doesn't matter.'

She'd given him a cold look. 'Dedicated to conservation? We'll leave that to the viewers to judge.'

The make-up girl had seemed amused when he sat down in front of a mirror and said something about having to give colour to most people but she'd have to tone his colour down. 'Where did you get that tan?' she had asked.

'Elsewhere. Here and there,' he had replied, and had almost added, 'not in your climate,' but that would have been misleading. It would have implied that he was a foreigner whereas he was English by birth and international only by inclination. There was no place he regarded as a home-town or dwelling he thought of as home. When he was younger he'd liked the sense of freedom provided by a nomadic way of life but with age he found himself increasingly wondering what it would be like to settle and have a permanent home.

In introducing him on the show, which was being televised live, the presenter had mentioned his world-wide travels and his present profession of trapping wild animals for zoos. 'But first,' she had said, turning to him with a smile, 'tell me, Paul, were you a bad boy at school or a conformist? I'd guess you resented authority. Right?'

She had virtually ignored him before the show but now she was smiling and calling him Paul. 'Paul' was only for people he knew well; otherwise he was Mr Phelan. And she was inviting him to agree with her which was a mistake. Until he had a measure of trust he never agreed with anyone for the sake of social nicety.

'Bad boy or conformist, are those the only alternatives?' he had asked. 'How about individualist?'

'You were an individualist?'

'Certainly. Expulsion from three schools should prove that.'

She had given a pretty, tinkling laugh. 'Three? I'll have to have a word with our researchers. They think there were four. But that's academic. Let's move on to the here and now. In your profession of big game hunter you've recently created something of a furore by trapping animals of an endangered species and selling them to a private zoo. Can you justify this except for the money?'

He had given himself time to think. The studio had become very quiet. Someone in the audience coughed.

'Is it the "big game hunter", the "endangered species" or the "private zoo" bit you want me to answer?'

'Let's take the private zoo bit. As I understand it, the Indian government are concerned that before rare animals are given an export licence there should be an undertaking that they will only go to zoos open to the general public. Right?'

'Absolutely right.'

8

'But you smuggled two extremely rare white tigers out of India and sold them to a private zoo. Is that correct?'

'I was commissioned by the owner of a private zoo to supply him with two white tigers, yes.'

'Perhaps you could tell us something about these beautiful and rare animals. Describe them.'

'Certainly.' As he spoke he saw a film of white tigers appear on a monitor and guessed they were the ones belonging to Bristol zoo. 'They have brownish grey stripes on an off-white background,' he said. 'They have bright blue eyes and their paws are pink. In the state of Rewa there have been only ten white tigers captured in the last fifty years. In neighbouring states a few others have been sighted. Animal rights groups and other fringe groups have made a big issue of the export of rare animals. My argument is that it's better to have them protected and cared for in a zoo, even a private zoo, than illegally killed to make a hearthrug for some millionaire.'

The moment he'd uttered the words he knew he'd given her an opening for attack. Her eyes glinted and her voice sharpened; she was a feline predator moving in for the kill.

'A hearthrug? But I believe you used to be a dealer in skins.'

Her researchers had done their work well, and they'd been right about the schools. He'd been expelled from four, not three.

'That was long ago and far away when I was younger. The skins I dealt in were mainly goat and sheep.'

'Not leopard?'

He smiled. He didn't have to answer simply because someone asked a question.

'Leopard skins for fur coats,' she went on, 'aren't much different from hearthrugs for millionaires.'

A leopard skin was how he'd come to meet the woman he'd married. He hoped the researchers hadn't unearthed this story.

'As I've said, that was long ago, about twenty years ago. I did deal in skins and I'm not ashamed of that, but I moved on to dealing in live animals.'

'Rare animals.'

'Sometimes.' He was glad she'd moved away from skin dealing. It was a time when he'd been taunted into killing a man, his wife had left him, and he'd gone native, living with a Barundi woman whose name he would never forget. Isabella.

She was asking another question. 'Tell me, how did you capture the white tigers?'

9

'The usual way. A pit. And then I tranquillised them.'

'But having done that, how did you get them out of India?'

'In a chartered aircraft. We crated them, loaded them and flew out. But don't ask who was with me, or where we flew from, or where we landed. Those matters are fairly sensitive.'

'Indeed. There are reports that there is a warrant being prepared for your arrest to stand trial in India and there are high-level diplomatic exchanges.'

He stretched his legs. A cameraman moved back. Another camera moved in. To his right he was aware of rows of faces. There was absolute silence. People in mass contracted into a knot of mute excitement when someone was about to be executed. He had once witnessed a beheading in Iran and had never heard such a terrible silence. It was as if everyone was holding breath and even nature had been halted; the world had stopped spinning.

When the silence was about to crack he said, 'What was that?'

An expression of anger flitted across her features and for a split-second she looked ten years older.

'I said there are reports that a warrant is being prepared for your arrest to stand trial in India. Would you like to comment on that?'

'I don't know where the reports come from, but I'm not worried. Britain doesn't have an extradition treaty with India.'

She drew back slightly like a cat about to pounce.

'You said you weren't ashamed of your days as a dealer in animal skins. Are you proud of stealing wild animals from their natural habitats for the private pleasure of a rich man?'

This was an easy question to answer. Very seriously he said, 'I am a dedicated conservationist. Believe it or not, I subscribe to the World Wildlife Fund. In my view human beings are not only the greatest predators on earth, they are the greediest. They don't take enough for what is necessary for survival, they take more than enough. The only way to protect endangered species against the greed of certain human beings is to have them safe in a zoological garden . . .'

'Behind bars,' she interrupted.

'No. In an environment as near as possible to their natural habitat.'

'You make it sound as though putting wild animals in captivity is some sort of service to them. Do you honestly think that being stuck in a crate, flown thousands of miles by air, and then being stuck in an unfamiliar environment is a service?'

'It's a service to their species. There has been some successful breeding in captivity of species which would have been as extinct as the dodo or the Tasmanian wolf.'

'Can you give some examples of that?'

'Certainly. In California the condor has been rescued from extinction by breeding at the San Diego zoo. The Arabian oryx is safe in a Jordanian reserve. The Hawaiian goose, Jackson's hartebeest, Madagascan angulated tortoises, the colobus monkey, the wattled crane, and many others have been saved from extinction.'

She looked puzzled. 'You say "saved", but for what purpose?'

He'd heard this question before and gave his standard reply. 'You tell me what purpose human beings serve and I'll tell you what purpose the wattled crane serves.'

She smiled. 'Right. Let's move back to the white tigers. I believe they are freaks. Not true tigers. An aberration. What's the point of perpetuating them?'

'I'm a hunter and a dealer, not a philosopher.'

'Let's look at it from another angle then. If the tigers had been obtained through legal channels, and were on view to the general public, that seems OK. But you got them surreptitiously for a private buyer, someone who's going to enjoy them to the exclusion of the public. You mentioned human greed, surely he's the most greedy of all.'

'That's something you could ask him, but I wouldn't recommend it.'

'Then may I ask you, is it really a desire to conserve on your part or is it simply that the money is good?' Before he could reply she added, 'What exactly are your motivations?'

He'd thought the programme was to be about conservation, not his motivations. But once embarked on a course he always saw it through, and he'd see this interview through even though he felt like walking out.

'Motivations? Money may be one. I don't think I'm greedy but, if I am, I'm no more greedy than someone who for money, and the power of the media, asks the sort of questions you're asking me. I try to conserve endangered species, and I do accept money for the risks I take. What's your excuse?'

'I don't need excuses, Mr Phelan. I'd suggest you were the one more in need of excuses, but our viewers are the best judges of that. Tell me, what's your next venture?'

He fought men with his fists and his brain but if you had to fight a woman you could only use brain. But whether it was a man or a woman, attack was the best method of defence.

'That's a very naive question,' he said. 'Do you really think I'm going to announce in public that I intend lifting a specified animal from the danger of extinction to the safety of a named, well-run zoo?'

Someone in the audience laughed and she laughed too as though he had cracked a joke.

'I was told beforehand that you were abrasive,' she replied, 'and you certainly are. I'd like to ask more but we're running out of time. Thank you.' She turned to the audience, 'Ladies and gentlemen, Mr Paul Phelan . . .'

There was a spatter of not very enthusiastic applause.

Recollecting the interview as he prowled around the cage he wondered about the programme researchers. There was much of his past they might have dug up if they'd known where to look, like the lost years spent after killing Verhaeren. The judicial enquiry had recorded a verdict of accidental death but he knew differently, and so did Murunga. He would never forget the look on his gun-bearer's face when he said, 'We both saw this cat at the same moment and fired.' Murunga had replied, 'I know. I saw the leopard. It ran between you both and disappeared into the trees.' There had been no leopard, and both knew it.

Although he had been born in England he had left when his father became manager of an overseas bank in Freetown, Sierra Leone. At the age of seventeen he had left a secure job in his father's bank to pursue his ambition to become a hunter. He crossed West Africa learning to track and kill various animals and then, financed by a Belgian Jew in Leopoldville, he went on an expedition to the unknown reaches of a tributary of the Congo. Here he discovered a tract of river which seethed with crocodile but after killing one hundred and seventy-nine his supply of hide-preserving salt was exhausted. Nevertheless he continued to kill crocodile until he possessed more than four hundred hides. But by the time he reached Leopoldville the unsalted hides were stinking and useless and some of the other hides hadn't been properly cleaned and were unsaleable. This

12

experience taught him never to be greedy when hunting and the lesson was a first step towards a distant and as yet unformulated desire to conserve wildlife.

After a period of hunting he decided to become a full-time dealer. Others could take the physical risks. He learned about the skin design of various animals, the patterns of interwoven fibres, and eventually became an expert. He had crossed and recrossed Africa adding to his store of knowledge when he met a man who offered him a partnership in a business operating in Ruanda-Urundi. It was here that he had met the woman who was to become his wife and where, for five twilight years after she had deserted him, he had sought solace in booze and the arms of a Bahutu woman called Isabella.

He was rescued from self-destruction by a Chinese Buddhist who was wandering through central Africa. He never discovered what such a man was doing in such a place. When he enquired he was given a conundrum in reply. 'Where else can one ride a tree as if it were a bicycle?' But although he never understood Buddhist riddles he learned that life should be respected and, if possible, preserved, and this included his own life.

He abandoned skin-dealing and became a hunter once more, not to kill but to save. His clients weren't always public zoos like the Antwerp zoo which specialised in Congo peacocks, or other advanced zoos like those in Washington or Sydney. Sometimes he sold to rich private buyers and this earned him the enmity of some animal welfare groups. Their hostility strengthened his belief, which no Buddhist doctrine could eliminate, that basically all men were enemies.

He stopped pacing the cage and because there was nowhere else to sit he sat down on the Elsan and waited. Sooner or later someone would come. If you take the trouble to capture an animal, whether it is a cheetah or a man, and you don't intend to kill it, you don't let it waste away unless you are in the business of maltreating political dissidents. Someone would eventually appear, but he wished they would soon come. He was hardened to temperature variables but protracted nakedness made him uncomfortable.

The only advantage of nakedness was that while giving away everything on one level, in a different sense you gave nothing except the information that you were male homo sapiens. Some

13

people felt diminished and insecure in this condition but Phelan's ego was too strong to be shaken in this way. Once more he tried to work out who might have brought him there.

He had arrived in England four days ago. The zoo owner had already arranged for facilities to conform to quarantine regulations and after delivering the two tigers Phelan had booked in at the Hilton hotel, intending to have a few days on the town before visiting a relative in Scotland. News of his exploit had been leaked to the media: it wasn't front page copy but was of sufficient interest to prompt irate letters in the correspondence columns and warrant an invitation to take part in a televised chat-show. There were press interviews and a meeting with Foreign Office officials.

Unaware of how long he had been unconscious, or what time of the day or night it was, the word 'yesterday' didn't have real meaning, but 'yesterday' evening, some twenty-four hours before the chat-show, he had gone to a bar in Soho, glad to escape from publicity. He had been on his second drink when a woman who was sitting on an adjoining stool produced a cigarette and asked him for a light.

'Sorry, I don't smoke,' he said.

'You don't? Then I won't.' She put away the cigarette.

He was amused. 'I'm not stopping you.'

'I know, and what's more you couldn't, could you? But if you're not smoking, I won't.'

She wore a low-cut black and green dress and leaf-shaped gold ear-clips. He estimated her age at about thirty; she had short fair hair, a pert nose and a wide mouth. He wasn't averse to casual encounters with pretty women. If sex was on offer, at a price or without, he occasionally accepted it. But, he flattered himself, he could take or leave sex, and if he took it there was always a clear understanding that no emotional involvement was intended. Since the break-up of his marriage he was determined never again to commit himself to any woman.

He asked if she'd like a drink.

'Thanks. Vodka and tonic with ice. Incidentally, my name is Cindy, if you want to know.'

Late that evening they went to her flat near Shepherd's Bush and the following morning she cooked him breakfast and said he could stay with her until he went to Scotland. Rather shyly she asked, 'Can I come with you to the studio? I've never been to a television studio.'

'Why not? We can go out for a meal after.'

That evening she had sat in the front row of the audience. He had declined the offer of the hospitality room when the interview had finished and they had left the studio to look for a taxi. As there wasn't one in sight they began to walk and it was then that the action started. Someone bumped against him on the sidewalk, a hand brushed his hip pocket, and the next moment a man was running away. Phelan gave chase, caught the man, regained his wallet and was about to give the thief something more physical than financial to remember him by when he was surrounded by a small throng of people, and that was the last he could recall.

He looked at the reddish patch on his arm. The pickpocket must have been a decoy and led him to a spot where someone in a group of people was able to jab him and then get him into a waiting car. It had been a carefully planned abduction.

What was Cindy doing now? Would she have raised the alarm? He was thinking about her when he heard a noise. A hooded figure in a loose sweater and jeans had appeared at the top of the staircase. Although the unknown person was wearing trainers, and could have been of either sex, Phelan guessed that his visitor was a woman.

She came slowly down the stairs followed by two similarly hooded figures. The third wore high-heeled shoes which clicked as she carefully picked her way down the stairs.

CHAPTER 2

They came to the cage and stood silently. He got off the Elsan and waited for them to speak; behind slits in the hoods he could just see the glint of their eyes. Silence prevailed and, unlike the bated-breath silence of a bloody execution, it was a peculiarly flat silence. He recognised different sorts of silence. There was the silence of the desert in which it seemed all sound had been vacuumed away, and the silence just before a storm on the veldt, but the silence he liked best was the silence of the night in the African bush which was no silence at all but a drone of millions of insects broken by the cries of nocturnal creatures. The present silence was odd because he felt he was part of a theatrical rehearsal in which a prolonged period of quiet was required in the stage directions. He waited for one of the trio to speak.

After a while he shrugged, turned and went to the mattress where he lay down on his back. If they wanted to stand and stare he preferred to recline at ease. The first figure turned to the other two and made a gesture with her hand. Phelan noticed that her left hand had a ring on every finger. Slowly, and in procession, they trooped away, mounted the stairs and disappeared. A door closed. He was alone once more.

People were kidnapped for political purposes, for obtaining ransom money, and for fund-raising student rags. He could rule out the political angle and, as for student rags, these were usually harmless capers and didn't involve drug injections. This left kidnapping for ransom, but who would pay to have him freed? Apart from Murunga and Isabella he couldn't think of a single person who would pay a cent for him. There might be one or two animals who, if they could think like human beings, would be willing to finance his freedom in return for his having provided them with a risk-free existence and regular meals in a custom-built sanctuary. And there were other animals whose

16

lives he had saved who might throw a few pennies into the ransom box.

One was a leopard saved from an excruciating death who owed him something. One day on his own in the bush he had come across three poachers who had snared the leopard. They had lighted a fire and were heating a poker. When it was red hot they intended pushing it up the leopard's anus, thereby inflicting an agonising death but preserving an unmarked coat. He had covered the men with a rifle and ordered one man to tie up the other two. Then he had fought the free man until the other was bleeding and unconscious. Next he had released a captive and fought him to a standstill. The third man had almost proved too tough but in the end he was senseless and, having thrashed the three, Phelan had unlocked the tiny cage which held the leopard. The cat, half crazy with fear, could have tried to maul him but it backed out of the cage, snarling and spitting, and turned to face him. For a few seconds its amber eyes and his grey eyes seemed magnetically locked. He held his rifle loosely by his side and might have got in one shot if the leopard had sprung but, still snarling, it had turned and loped away. It was ridiculous, and unprovable, but he knew the leopard and he had understood each other.

In gratitude the leopard would have forced his captors to release him, just as in a different act of gratitude a lion had once saved the life of the slave Androcles.

He stood up and stretched his limbs.

'If you're listening,' he said, 'and I expect you are, I could do with a whisky. A malt, preferably.'

He hadn't expected an immediate reaction but a voice came through the cavity at the top of the stairs.

'Yes, we're listening. And watching. What does it feel like to be a caged animal, and watched?'

So that was the answer. Some animal liberation group or anti-zoo nutters were punishing him for earning a living by capturing wild animals and bringing them, and their species, to safety. The voice belonged to a woman. He had been right. His captors were women.

'How does it feel,' the voice continued, 'to have been tranquillised like you tranquillise your victims?'

'I get it,' he said. 'You're trappers.'

'Trappers using your methods.'

I don't go around wearing a hood. But maybe you're from outer space and the hoods are to disguise your bug eyes.'

'Why are you trying to be funny? Why the schoolboy humour? Or is it macho humour? Are you trying to keep up your spirits? Are you afraid?'

'I'm not afraid of three bloody women,' he retorted.

'That's a sexist remark, but I could have guessed you were sexist as well as speciesist. You're probably a racist too.'

He didn't laugh, but Murunga and Isabella would certainly have laughed if they'd been told what the woman meant. The only discrimination Phelan practised was against snobs of whatever colour or race. As for sexism, he was no different from the creatures of the wild who possessed innate recognition of the fundamental differences between male and female. Try teaching a Rwanda baboon to accept a female into his male hierarchy!

But he wouldn't argue. He'd had enough of that with the TV show presenter.

'You have an apartheid mentality, Mr Phelan. Discriminate, segregate. Apartheid doesn't exist only in South Africa.'

'I don't know what you look like,' he said. 'Maybe you're a dish, but you would as sure as hell bore the pants off any man.'

A faint intake of breath came over the loudspeaker. 'I'm sorry you find my conversation boring. I'll leave you to your more interesting thoughts. Good day.'

He didn't reply. It didn't matter that she had gone off the air; he had learned something about his captors, and her farewell 'Good day' was an indication that in the outside world it was day, not night. How long had he been unconscious?

Without his watch or the sun or stars to measure the passing of time it was difficult to estimate duration. He had once been trapped in a cave and when rescued had thought a whole day must have passed. To his astonishment it was almost two days.

If he was right in thinking some animal rights group was responsible for his predicament, what did they hope to gain? Perhaps it was sufficient for them to submit him to the humiliation of being naked and caged. They were attempting to make this punishment fit the crime of capturing wild animals, but they didn't understand that he and they were on the same side, the side of animals threatened by humankind.

The silence was shattered by high-pitched squeals, the sound of animals in pain. It was amplified to almost deafening volume before being faded out. A woman, through the loudspeaker,

18

said, 'That's the sound of a seal cull, Mr Phelan. I expect, as a hunter, you enjoyed it.'

Was it worth telling her he no longer hunted to kill and, anyway, had never hunted or clubbed seals? No, it wasn't.

After a pause, the recording was played again and cries of animal agony tore into the cellar's acoustics. He was forced to put his hands over his ears. Eventually the aural battering stopped and the benediction of silence returned.

Although it was ridiculous to link his trade with seal culling he could begin to see that to an extremist there was a connection between the two. As he began to consider the arguments for and against his trade he began to feel drowsy, his mind freewheeled, and it was an effort not to fall asleep. He wondered what drug had been used to knock him out; it certainly had after-effects. He didn't feel himself. It wasn't simply a physical difference; he was analysing his own motivations, something he didn't normally do. But this was the effect of disorientation on a man. Get him into an alien environment, sap his energies, and you could make him question himself. This was the basis of brainwashing.

For some time he had been increasingly aware of a need to urinate. He stood up. 'Watch this, girls,' he said. After a bold flourish in the direction of the ventilator shaft he directed a stream against the metal interior of the Elsan. Having relieved himself he began prowling round the cage once more. He was no longer thinking about the reason for his kidnapping; he was consumed by a desire for revenge. Once free he wouldn't rest until his captors had been made to suffer for putting him through a degrading ordeal.

The molten fury of his anger subsided and left a residue of cold determination to exact retribution. He stopped pacing. What next? He was a man who disliked prolonged physical inactivity; he needed stimulus. It was boring and unproductive to lie on the mattress but scarcely less boring to continue pacing the narrow confines of the cage. For a while he occupied himself by using the bars for isometric exercises; then he ran on the spot but, realising that his penis flapping up and down might provide any female watcher with an opportunity for ridicule, he did some press-ups. As he did so he remembered what a randy croc hunter had once told him. 'You do a dozen press-ups every morning and you'll be fit for the missionary position in the evening.'

When his muscles were aching he lay down on the mattress

and went through some relaxation exercises but although his body responded at first, tension returned when he began to wonder who had set him up. Was it Cindy, and was she a member of an animal rights outfit? She liked big cats. In her sitting room there was a reproduction from a painting by Donald Grant which showed a cheetah standing on a rock in the Masai Mara as it scanned a rugged landscape for prey.

His thoughts turned to the TV presenter. It was highly unlikely that she was involved in the abduction but she'd made it clear she disapproved of his trade. He couldn't remember her name; she might be a household name to the millions who fed on television pap but to him she was someone who for a few minutes had been an anonymous irritant.

A sense of frustration suddenly swept over him and he had to resist an urge to shout obscenities at his captors. The fury faded and he was aware of a tickle on his chin. Fingering his face, he felt a ridge of stubble. He had often been obliged to come to terms with the absence of elementary necessities of hygiene when camping out in arid regions and had frequently gone for days without using a razor. When water was strictly rationed he preferred cleaning his teeth to having a wet shave. As his fingers delicately traced a line between chin and ear he estimated that the beard was at least a day old.

It was during his facial reconnaissance that the door at the top of the stairs opened and a hooded figure appeared carrying a bottle which he instantly recognised as a liquor he bought regularly at duty-free shops, Grant's Glenfiddich malt whisky.

The hooded woman came up to the cage and as he began to move towards her she said, 'Stay where you are, or you won't get this. It's what you asked for.'

'How kind. Your hospitality disarms me.'

She pushed the bottle through the cage bars. 'Sarcastic sod,' she said.

'No glass? A good malt requires cut crystal at least.'

'Drink from the bottle, baby.'

'I will, but why the maternal concern?'

She turned and walked away without answering, mounted the stairs and slammed the door behind her.

The bottle was almost full. He put it to his lips and took a lick. The taste was authentic Glenfiddich malt. He took a swig and almost at once his veins seemed to expand with relief. Another swig, and as he clasped the bottle he realised he'd been provided with a weapon, a club. He took another drink, a long pull and wiped his mouth with the back of his hand rubbing the skin hard against a sandpaper moustache. The gesture might have been too violent because he experienced a moment's unsteadiness. With the consciously deliberate gait of someone who wishes to demonstrate perfect control in spite of being slightly drunk he went to the Elsan, put down the lid and squatted. Seated, he felt better, steadier. For a few minutes he nursed the bottle and then, as if by an unthinking reflex, he lifted it to his mouth once more.

The bars of the cage seemed to shift. He screwed up his eyes. The bars moved slowly to the left and then to the right. No food, too much to drink, I'm getting pissed, he thought. Very carefully he placed the bottle on the floor. A moment later the door opened. He watched, bemused, as three figures descended the stairs. This time there was a difference in apparel.

The first two were dressed as before in loose sweaters and jeans, but the third wore a black mask, a skimpy black bra which made her breasts pout, black panties, suspenders, fishnet stockings and high-heeled ankle-strap shoes. In her left hand she carried a long whip.

He couldn't take his eyes off her. What the hell were they playing at? He stood up and almost keeled over. His legs felt like paper and his head was swimming in a haze. The whisky must have been topped up with something more potent which hadn't destroyed its taste.

The first woman reached the cage door. She unlocked the padlock and the door swung open. This was his opportunity. He reached for the bottle and fell over. One of the women gave a harsh laugh. With a great effort he managed to stand upright. 'What's the idea?' he asked, and he could hear his own voice unnaturally slurred so that the words came out as 'Wash idea.'

The women in sweaters took up a position by the door and the third woman entered the cage. 'Stand back,' she ordered and the whip lashed and cracked inches from his face.

'This is a man-training session,' she said. 'You are going to find out what it's like to be one of the animals you trap.' The whip was raised to strike. 'Stand back or you'll get it where it hurts most.'

He shifted back unsteadily. 'You spiked my drink.'

'It's only what you deserve. The animals you sell into

21

captivity get drugged before they're made to perform.'

It was almost painful to concentrate his mind but he managed to say, 'I've never sold to circuses.'

'Maybe not, but some of the animals you've trapped have ended their days in misery in cheap circuses, forced to climb on to stools and platforms.'

'So what?'

'So you're going to be put through your paces. Get up.'

He was bewildered. 'Get up?'

With the whip handle she indicated the Elsan. 'Stand on that. Stand on the box like a good lion.'

'To hell with that.'

The whip flashed and its tip stung the flesh of his left thigh.

'Now do as you're told. Next time it'll be closer to what you most treasure. In case you've got any doubts, I'm expert at this treatment.'

It was difficult to keep his balance even though his feet were planted apart. He swayed drunkenly, arms hanging loosely, mouth gaping and eyes screwed up. He looked more like a primitive anthropoid than twentieth-century man.

The whip cracked as it snaked past his face. He jerked back and almost fell. One of the women by the door laughed.

'Hurry,' said the ring-mistress. 'I don't like to be kept waiting. My sort don't.' She pointed the whip at the Elsan. 'Get up, or suffer for disobedience.'

He turned his head to look at the Elsan. It seemed to shift sideways. 'How can I? The damn thing is on wheels.'

'You'll have weals if you don't do as you're told. Up! Up! Up!'

He faced his tormentor. Behind the slits in her mask two eyes glittered. The bitch is enjoying herself, he thought, and he was aware of the pain in his thigh where the lash had struck. His drink had been spiked, the odds were against him, but if he managed to get on to the Elsan he might be able to jump on her. He said, 'You'll pay for this.'

'You'll pay for this,' she mimicked. 'How original! How subtle!' The timbre of her voice hardened. 'Don't try to be macho with me, you pathetic two-legged apology of a man. Now get up!'

He lifted a leg and put his foot on the Elsan lid.

'Good boy. Now the other one.'

22

Flexing his muscles he hoisted the other leg, teetered uncertainly, flailed his arms in an effort to retain balance, saw the room spin round him, reeled sideways and fell with a thud to the floor.

She came and stood over his prone body, legs astride his waist. 'Now you're where you belong. On the floor. Crawling.'

'I'm not crawling.'

Beneath the mask her mouth smirked. 'Don't argue with me or I'll make you lick my boots.'

'What do you want?' he asked. His speech was still slightly slurred but the cellar had stopped spinning. He was overcoming the intoxication but the bottle was out of reach and the whip was swishing above him.

'We want an apology.'

'Apology. What for?'

'For your life-style, for the cruelty of stealing wild animals, and before I've finished with you you'll be begging to make an apology in writing, and signed. We shall circulate copies and make sure it gets the fullest possible publicity and then, and only then, we might consider releasing you.'

It might have been due to the shock of his fall but his mind was clearing and his thoughts were no longer disconnected. He was capable of planning an escape. He shifted so that his hands were close to her ankles and as he did this he said, 'OK, I'll do that. But first tell me what's the idea of the fancy dress?'

She jabbed at his chest with the whip handle. 'I've a good mind to punish you for that.'

His hands were almost touching her ankles. He was ready to put his plan into action. First he must anger her so that she'd raise her whip arm to lash him. In that moment, while her shoulders were back, he'd grab her ankles and pull. She would fall backwards, he'd dive for the bottle, and with this weapon he could take on the three of them.

He looked up at the masked face. 'One more question,' he said.

'What?'

'Are you the only whore or are the other two whores as well?'

Her lips tightened and the whip began to swish. 'You'll be sorry for that.'

'Sorry,' he jeered. 'You couldn't make me sorry. You're just a whore who's full of hot air.'

23

She raised her arm and in the split-second that she was slightly off balance he seized her ankles and pulled. She seemed to shimmy, a vibration passed through her body as if she was in some earth-rooted dance, and then, like a felled silver birch, black and flesh-white, she toppled over.

As she keeled backwards he rolled sideways, released his grip and made a grab for the bottle. But he misjudged distances and the heel of her right shoe struck his face. Before he could recover one of the other women was on top of him. He felt something needle-sharp pierce his arm just above the elbow. It was his bad luck that the point of a syringe hit a vein and within two seconds he was fighting a fuzz of drowsiness; within five seconds he was unconscious.

CHAPTER 3

He gazed up at a crescent moon framed by a serrated outline of tree foliage. It was a night in late September and he had surfaced through a vivid dream of being in a snowdrift clad only in a string vest. Before the dream faded he had fleetingly wondered about the vest: he never wore vests, let alone string vests.

He was lying on his back. As he sat up and his eyes adjusted to the darkness he saw a heap of clothing by his feet. Looking around he realised he was in a wood; a distant hum of engine noise meant he was fairly close to a main road. The women must have brought him here and dumped him. For some reason they must have given up the idea of making him write and sign an apology for trading in animals.

He got to his feet and began to dress. When he slipped on his jacket he was glad to find his passport and wallet, both of which he always carried, were still there. At least the women weren't thieves; they hadn't even taken an authorisation from the Zimbabwe government to export one male black rhino.

He breathed deeply and began to swing his arms to promote circulation but had to stop when he felt a pain in his back. When he was fully dressed he made his way towards the sound of road traffic. Soon he was at the edge of the wood and he could see the lights of fast-moving vehicles.

As he walked towards the road he wondered what action to take. He would try to hitch a lift, but to where? His first thought was to ask to be taken to a police station but if he reported what had happened he wouldn't be able to operate freely to exact revenge. The rule of law would prevail and he preferred the law of the jungle. As a young man he had once presided over a kangaroo court which had tried a porter for stealing and selling badly needed provisions. Technically the man should have been reported to the police once a town was reached but instead he was strung up to a tree, arms above head, and flogged. He had accepted his punishment without complaint and resumed his duties. The matter was never reported.

Phelan was also deterred by pride from going to the police. He wasn't easily embarrassed but the thought of giving details of his ordeal to a duty officer, possibly a uniformed female, added an extra chill to the night air. Apart from this, he preferred to settle his own problems without assistance from anyone else and, in any event, the police would have no better idea than he where his captors had held him. Since he couldn't describe their faces there couldn't be an identification parade. He would use his own methods of tracking and retribution.

Countless cars and long-distance trucks passed him as he tried to thumb a lift but at last a small car slowed down.

A young man wound down the passenger window. 'What's the trouble, mate?'

'My car's broken down,' said Phelan.

'I didn't see no car.'

'No. I pulled off the road. Can you give me a lift to civilisation? I'm not sure where I am.'

'You're on the road to Epping.' The door was unlocked. 'Hop in. I'll take you there.'

He was a mini-cab driver and had been hired to collect a customer from a party.

'The guy didn't fancy drinking and driving. Good for him and good for me.'

Phelan didn't reply. He didn't want to encourage small talk. At the best of times he found casual conversation unproductive and boring, and this wasn't the best of times. Moreover, he didn't want to be recognised; the driver might have seen him on television. Turning his head he saw the dark outline of trees; this stretch of road must run through Epping Forest.

He leaned forward to use the lights on the dashboard to check the time on his watch and then remembered that his watch had been taken away. He felt in his pockets but failed to find it.

'Lost something, mate?' enquired the driver.

'No.'

The clock on the car dashboard showed it was almost midnight.

A note of curiosity entered the man's voice. 'Been travelling far?'

'Quite a way.'

26

'What sort of car have you got then?'

'Saab.'

'Never driven a Saab. Has it got fuel injection?'

Phelan hesitated before saying, 'Yes.' He wished the driver would shut up.

The wish wasn't granted. 'I could drop you off at a garage where they have a twenty-four-hour recovery service. Are you with the AA or RAC?'

'If you could drop me near a call-box I'd be grateful.'

'Sure. No problem.'

A car came towards them with headlights on beam. The young man flashed his own lights. 'Some people have got no thought for others,' he said. 'They think they're kings of the road.'

'How far are we from Epping?'

'About a couple of miles. What was the cause of the breakdown then?'

'I don't know. The engine cut.'

'But you could pull off. Maybe you just ran out of petrol.'

'Maybe.'

'I did that once. Had a bird with me. She thought it was a put-up job and scorched my ears. Said she wasn't that sort of girl. I told her I wasn't that sort of fella. It was what you might call a confrontation. But there was a happy ending.' He paused, waiting for Phelan to show interest in the ending. None was forthcoming. 'Have a guess at what the ending was then.'

Phelan was in no mood for guessing. 'You'd been having a bad dream,' he said.

'No. This was for real. I'll tell you. We got engaged and then we married, and now the wife's in the club.'

Phelan wanted to kill all conversation dead. He said, 'Where's the happy ending? I thought you said there was a happy ending? Sounds bloody awful to me.'

The man beside him stiffened. 'Look, mate, I done you a favour, and I don't think that's a very nice thing to say.'

From this point on both men looked rigidly and silently ahead. When a row of houses came into view the driver slowed down and pulled into an empty bus-stop.

'There's a call-box just down the road,' he said brusquely. 'You can get out.'

'Right.'

Phelan regretted his intolerant remark about happy endings,

27

not because he was being offloaded, but he didn't like gratuitous rudeness in anyone, including himself, and he had been less than polite to a man who had helped him. He took out his wallet and produced a note. 'Here you are, and thanks for the lift.'

'You can stuff that,' said the driver.

Phelan put the note away and got out. The car was driven away with a ferocity that made the tyres screech. Fluorescent lamps threw sickly light on to a deserted street. For a few moments he debated whether to find accommodation for the night, to see if he could find a car hire firm willing to take him to central London, or to find a railway station and wait for the first train out. He began walking and when he found the call-box he paused and then continued walking. He'd had enough of publicity. At first it had been a novelty and a challenge but now it was burdensome. The night wasn't too cold, he'd find a hollow and doss down for a few hours. It wouldn't be the first time he'd slept rough. At daybreak he'd make his way to town and catch a train to London.

On impulse he turned around to walk back towards the country. The sudden movement caused a momentary pain in his back. It was quickly forgotten and he began to wonder what day of the week it was. In the morning he'd buy a newspaper and find out; at a guess he thought the abduction had taken two days out of his life.

He was correct. Approximately fifty-two hours had passed from the time of the kidnap until he was picked up by the mini-cab driver. He reached his hotel while most other guests were enjoying breakfast. He collected his room key and two letters which were awaiting him. His first and most imperative need was a shower. It was after he had stripped off that he examined his back in the bathroom mirror. Three red weals ran from right shoulder to waist. They were tender to the touch and he couldn't think what had caused the marks unless they were the result of being dragged across rough ground.

After showering and shaving he put on fresh clothes, picked up the letters and went to the restaurant; he was very hungry. After giving his order, he ripped open two envelopes, one white and one mauve. The letter in the white envelope was anonymous abuse in which he was unfavourably likened to a depraved psychopath who relished tormenting animals. He tore the letter into fine shreds which were placed in an ashtray. The other letter, on deckle-edged mauve paper, with address embossed in green, was brief and breath-catching.

Dear Paul,

Surprise? Surprise? I was surprised to see your weather-beaten visage on the box last night. If I may say so, you have aged very handsomely. I haven't done too badly either – or so my devoted husband tells me! If you have time before moving on we'd love to see you. How about dinner one evening? At least, give me a call and tell me how things really are with you.

Yours ever – if that doesn't seem too ironic,

Karen (Ormerod)

Karen Ormerod had once been Karen Phelan and was the writer of travel books and romantic novels under the pseudonym of Karen Fitzwilliams. Eighteen years had passed since their divorce. From time to time he had seen her name on the spine of a book and had once taken a copy from the shelf of a ship's library during a boring voyage across the Indian Ocean. According to the blurb it was a gothic romance written after the author had visited the prison of Pignerola on the island of Sainte Marguerite. Phelan had found the story implausible but had been fascinated by the description of the heroine's wicked jailer; it was a perfect portrait of his old enemy, Verhaeren. And the man who rescued her although not resembling himself physically had been given his name, Paul. He had forgotten the book's title but remembered that he'd never finished it because he'd joined a poker school and this had been a more entertaining way of passing time.

For a few minutes the letter erased thoughts of revenge from his mind but after breakfast he hired a taxi to Shepherd's Bush. Cindy's flat number was forty-two but he wasn't sure of the address. 'It's Green something,' he said to the cab driver.

'That'll be Greenhill Mansions,' replied the driver. 'I took a fare there the other night.'

The block of flats looked vaguely familiar but when he rang the bell of number forty-two the door was opened by a square-jawed woman wearing a crimson house-coat tied at the waist by a brown cord.

'I'm looking for someone called Cindy,' said Phelan.

The woman shook her head. 'You've come to the wrong place, dear. No one of that name here.'

'Three nights ago I was here with her.'

'Sorry, dear, you must have made a mistake. I've been here five years and I don't know anyone of that name.'

He peered past her into the hallway and saw an umbrella stand and a carved oak chest, neither of which had been in Cindy's flat.

'You must be on the wrong floor,' the woman continued. 'And now you must excuse me. I'm busy.' She closed the door.

Phelan stood for a few moments deep in thought. Although the lay-out of the block was familiar there was something different. The elevator shaft was in the wrong place and the corridor carpeting was of a different colour and material, facts he hadn't noticed in his hurry to reach number forty-two.

Outside it had started to rain heavily. He decided to return to his hotel and telephone his ex-wife; the search for Cindy could be temporarily postponed.

Back in his room he dialled her number. When she answered he said, 'Paul here.'

He heard a sharp intake of breath. 'I'm so glad you called. I was beginning to think you wouldn't.'

'How are you, Karen?'

'I'm fine. What about you?'

'Fine.' He felt strangely tongue-tied.

'Good. I'd love to see you. Any chance of your coming round tonight? I know it's short notice but tomorrow we've got something on, and the next day we're off to America. I've got a promotional tour.'

During their short married life they had spent a few weeks in London and he had met some of her friends. He spoke English, they spoke English, but under the surface of spoken language there was little communication. To them he was an interesting exhibit, Karen's latest, and to him they were insincere and pretentious. He had never felt at ease during those weeks in London and now the same feeling, of being a fish out of water, returned at the sound of her voice.

'Are you there, Paul?'

'Yes.'

'Well, can you come round tonight?'

'I'd like to . . . very much.'

'How about seven thirty for eight? We live in a quiet little

30

cul-de-sac not far from Kensington High Street.'

'I'll find it.' His voice was shorn of social pleasantry; he might have been speaking to a rival animal trapper and, in a sense, he was. Karen trapped, took what she wanted from her prey, and moved on.

Her laugh came down the line. 'I'm sure you'll find it. I haven't forgotten how we found Kitega. Remember?'

He seldom liked being reminded of the past. Past was past. He lived for the present and future. Some men might have replied, 'How could I forget?' or 'That was something to remember'; he simply said, 'Yes.'

'Dear Paul. Laconic as ever. It'll be lovely to see you again. Bye.'

He was left holding a phone on a dead line just as he had been left in Africa when Karen had walked out on him after the business with Verhaeren. He didn't brood on what was past but sometimes in dreams, and he was a man haunted by dreams; he would enter the room she had used as a writing room and find her there, her fingers dancing on a typewriter. She would look up at him and smile and he would say, 'So you didn't leave me. It was a mistake.' These dreams, less frequent in recent years, were in some ways more disturbing than the nightmares of being savaged by Verhaeren wearing a leopard mask.

He replaced the phone. Almost at once it rang.

'This is reception, Mr Phelan. There's someone from the press. Shall I send him up?'

'No. Tell him I'm not available, and tell anyone else the same thing. OK?'

'Certainly, sir.'

He should have followed his instincts and shunned publicity from the start but he wasn't ashamed of his trade and he had a genuine desire to put the record straight. He wasn't a common poacher; he was a conservationist and future generations would be grateful to men like him.

He lay down on the bed and closed his eyes. He wished he was back in Africa; he wished he was anywhere but London, England, a place where the memories, if one cared to look back, were mainly bad. Within seconds he was asleep.

He woke with a start and looked at the place on his wrist where his watch should have been strapped. Then he remembered. It had been stolen, the one item the women had taken. He

31

called up reception and asked the time. He was told, 'Six thirty-seven.'

In an hour's time he was due at Karen's. He slid off the bed and went to the bathroom.

CHAPTER 4

After opening the front door she had kissed him lightly on the cheek, given a penetrating stare and said, 'You look even better than you did on TV.'

He told her of the make-up girl's remark about his complexion needing to be toned down.

She laughed and the years slipped away. He might have just arrived home after a day in the warehouse in Usumbura. She hadn't changed much. Fine lines had appeared at the corners of her eyes and her fair hair had a few threads of silver.

She had got him a drink and they went through a sitting room, out of open french windows, and into a small garden enclosed by a high wall. Most of the ground area was covered by flagstones but there was one bed filled with miniature flowering shrubs. An old mimosa tree spread delicate branches over one corner of the house.

'It's not very big,' said Karen, 'but it suits us. The disadvantage is that the garden only gets about an hour's direct sunlight and you know how I like the sun. On the other hand, it's marvellously private and no one would think we were in the heart of London.' She gave him an oblique look. 'In case you're wondering where Dennis is, he'll be home soon. He's playing squash. A physical man.'

'How long have you been married?'

She shrugged. 'I don't know. Who's counting? What about you? Did you ever . . .'

He shook his head.

'Was once enough?' She held up a hand. 'Don't answer that.'

He hadn't intended to answer. He had never been adept at slick one-liners and the alternative would have been a laboured denial.

She switched the conversation back to the garden and he was

glad to discuss light and shade, soil quality and plant life. She picked up a hose and began spraying a tub of geraniums. 'I have to water each day,' she said, 'so little rain gets through.'

'But you like it here?' The question was tinged with disbelief.

'It's a base in London. We have another place in Florida and we travel a lot.'

'Still writing?'

'Oh, yes. And selling, I'm happy to say. What about you?'

He gave a brief résumé of life since their parting, glossing over the wasted years when he had gone native and not mentioning the travelling Buddhist who had rescued him from apathetic indifference.

They were in the sitting room having a second drink when Dennis Ormerod appeared. He was about the same height as Phelan and had the look of an outdoor man. Karen, a small and dainty woman, had always been attracted by men who behaved like stereotypes of men's men; keen on sport, never completely at ease in female company, equipped with mechanical know-how but generally short on appreciation of the arts; men who would sooner listen to a night club singer than watch grand opera, preferred Ernest Hemingway to James Joyce, and thought abstract art was a con trick played on a gullible public.

After a few minutes Karen said, 'I must check how things are going. Won't be a moment.'

Dennis Ormerod braced himself, pectoral muscles expanding under an open-neck check shirt. He looked what he was, a man who was about to play the part of host and do his duty by making polite enquiries of his guest, a complete stranger who, in a curious way, was no stranger because Karen had sometimes spoken of Phelan and her life with him.

'I don't watch television,' he said. 'Think it rather a waste of time.'

'So do I,' said Phelan.

'You do? Karen quite likes it and I have to say we saw you the other night. Thought you came out of it well, but then I can't stick the self-opinionated bitch who runs the show.'

'Nor could I. What's her name? Nan something, isn't it?'

'Nan Bellman. A women's libber. They say she's going to change her name to Nan Bellperson.'

'That's a name I shall commit to memory,' said Phelan.

'We met her at a party a couple of weeks ago. She was saying some really bitchy things about a rival presenter.'

They were still discussing the TV show when Karen returned and sat on the arm of her husband's chair. 'What are we talking about?' she asked.

'Nancy Bellperson.'

She grimaced. 'Can't we change the subject? I don't want to get indigestion.' She turned to Paul. 'How are things in the dark continent? I've been reading some dreadful stories about ivory poachers.'

He told them that not only was the elephant at risk but out of twenty-five thousand black rhinos only three hundred were left. There wasn't only a market for rhino horns as aphrodisiacs but the Yemenis paid high prices to have them for dagger handles.

'This is getting depressing again,' said Karen, 'let's have dinner. Are you hungry, Paul?'

'Very. I haven't eaten too well the last two or three days.'

'No? Why's that?'

'It's a long story.'

It wasn't until the meal was almost finished and Karen had produced a bowl of fruit and a board of cheese that she said, 'I do believe you really were hungry. Are you going to tell us the long story?'

Inhibited by an ingrained reluctance to give away anything personal, he didn't answer immediately. Karen and Dennis Ormerod waited as he weighed up whether to tell them of the ordeal. He didn't want sympathy, but he felt a need to talk about the experience to someone trustworthy.

'Go on,' said Karen softly.

'I don't want this to go any further.'

'It won't.'

He gave a wry grin. 'Not even in disguise in a novel?'

She crossed her heart with her hand. 'I promise.'

Haltingly, picking his words as though he were treading through a semantic minefield, he told of the kidnap and imprisonment in a cage, omitting only the fact that he had been totally naked. He abbreviated the sequence where a whip had been cracked, although he did describe the woman's gear. As he listed the garments he heard Karen give a little gasp; this surprised him as she wasn't the sort of woman to be shocked by such details.

He explained how he had thrown the woman off balance and

then been jabbed by one of the others, and how he had come to consciousness lying on the ground looking up at the moon. He'd managed to hitch a lift to the town of Epping, two or three miles away. He finished by saying, 'I'm not going to rest until I've found them.'

'How are you going to set about that?' Karen asked.

He told them of Cindy and how he suspected her complicity in the plot, and he mentioned the abortive search for her flat.

'Will you try again to find it?' Karen asked.

'I might, or I might go to the bar where we met. At the moment, I'm not sure.'

'What about your visit to Scotland?'

'I've postponed it.'

Dennis Ormerod who had been silent throughout the narrative turned to Karen and said, 'Could be a job for Samson.'

She nodded. 'Maybe ... Paul, there was something you said about the woman with the whip. The way she was dressed. Would you describe her as someone who might deliver a kissogram?'

'Kissogram?'

'You know, sexy gear. Black lingerie and flashing bare thighs. Pin-up fodder for soldiers on duty in a god-forsaken hole. The centrefold of soft porn mags.'

'Yes. That fits.'

'And you were on the fringe of Epping Forest, about two or three miles south of the town?'

'That's right. Why?'

'Only earlier tonight, while I was getting the meal ready, I had the radio on. I was listening to LBC, that's a station which broadcasts news in and around London. One of the news items was about a woman's body found this morning a few miles south of Epping.'

In the hush following her statement Dennis Ormerod cut a slice of Brie. 'How about a glass of port?' he asked Phelan.

'Thanks, yes ... I don't get it, Karen. What's the connection?'

'There was a short interview with the man who found her. He has two dogs he exercises before going off to work in the City. He works on the Stock Exchange and said that the other day, his birthday, some colleagues arranged for a kissogram to be delivered while they were having a pub lunch. He came across this body and said that for a moment he thought some ghastly joke was being played on him and it was the same girl. She was dressed the same way. Then he realised she was dead. She was wearing a black mask.... Was the woman with the whip wearing a mask?'

Ormerod placed a glass of port by Phelan.

'Yes.'

'Then it's either a coincidence or it was her.'

When something hit you out of the blue you didn't show concern; you displayed indifference. Phelan took a sip of port. 'Very good,' he said, and he cut a slice of cheese, slowly and deliberately, as if taking a piece of Brie was the most important act of his life.

'I hope it is a coincidence,' said Karen, 'and you're not being fitted up.'

'Fitted up for what?'

Impatience swept across her face. 'For a moment,' she said, 'just forget what reviewers have said of me. That I have a vivid imagination. You are at the receiving end of an incident so bizarre that some people wouldn't believe it. You finally surface in a wood. It happens to be close to the place where someone who is dressed like a woman who featured in the bizarre incident is found dead. Either it is an extraordinary coincidence or you're being fitted up for murder. Suppose you hadn't recovered when you did. Suppose you'd recovered around the time this man took his dogs for a walk. Where would you be now? At a guess I'd say you'd be with the police being closely questioned.'

'Who'd want to fit me up, and why?'

'I don't know.'

'This Cindy girl. Was she a prostitute?'

'I'm not sure.'

'Not sure?' Karen exclaimed. 'You must be. Did you pay her?'

Phelan very nearly told her to mind her own business but he choked back this instant retort and said, 'I gave her a present of money. But she seemed a bit surprised, almost as if she hadn't expected it. But yes, I'd say she was a pro. She was on her own in this bar and she started the talk by asking for a light. If that isn't a standard opening, what is?'

Karen didn't reply.

'Why don't we watch the ten o'clock news,' said Ormerod, 'and see if there's anything on it. The dead woman might have been the kissogram girl.'

'She wasn't,' Karen replied. 'That was how the news item

37

finished. She'd been traced and was very much alive.' She turned to Phelan. 'Would you like to watch the ten o'clock news?'

'If you want to, I don't mind.'

'You won't admit, even to yourself, that it's a very strange coincidence that after being knocked out by a drug you should come to near a place where a dead body is found? Aren't you interested in following it up?'

'I'm interested in finding out who pushed me around. And when I do, God help them.'

'Well, I'm going to watch the news.' She began to stand and then sat down again. 'When you've finished eating,' she concluded.

He pushed his plate aside. 'I've finished.'

'Coffee?'

'That'd be fine.'

A few minutes later they were in the sitting room watching a television newscast. It lasted half an hour and no mention was made of the discovery of a woman's body.

'It's not national news,' said Karen. 'There are so many these days that only the spectacular make the headlines. And in the LBC programme they said she hadn't been sexually interfered with. It's a dull murder when sex isn't involved.'

'That's a bit cynical, darling,' protested Ormerod.

'It's a realistic comment.' She turned to Phelan. 'Haven't you thought of reporting what happened to the police?'

'I don't want to do things legally.'

She gave him a curious look. 'You want revenge, don't you?'

'Yes. It may be uncivilised, but I'm not altogether sold on civilisation.'

'It was the same with . . .' She stopped short of naming Verhaeren, but he understood.

'Yes,' he said, 'it was the same.'

'What's that?' asked Ormerod.

'Oh, nothing,' Karen chipped in before Phelan could reply. 'It's just that I remember that once Paul gets his heart set on something, heaven help anyone who stands in his way.'

Ormerod pondered her statement before giving his opinion. 'I think you should engage Samson, Paul. Get him to sniff out who was responsible for what happened to you. It might throw some light on the woman who was found today.'

'Who is Samson?'

Husband and wife looked at each other. 'You tell him,' said

38

Karen. 'But it's something that doesn't get any further than this room, Paul.'

He crossed his heart, imitating her action earlier. 'I promise.'

Ormerod took over. 'A couple of years ago we were in Marseilles. Karen was researching for a book on Provence. One evening she was out for a walk and simply disappeared. It was only much later I discovered she'd been attacked from behind by someone she didn't know. Karen was knocked out. When she recovered she wandered around in a state of concussion and drifted into the Arab quarter. She was taken in by a couple of Algerians. Like you, she was a prisoner. The police wouldn't help me. They'd enough crime on their hands without looking for an Englishwoman who, for all they knew, might have left the town of her own accord. I got a chap from England, a private investigator called John Samson, and thank God he was successful in finding Karen. Mind you, I didn't take to him at first. A fat, lazy-looking fellow. And a bit eccentric. He had an obsession with Time; Time spelled with a capital "T". But he did his stuff. I'd recommend him to anyone. He could be the man for you, Paul.'

Phelan said, 'I'll take a note of his address before I go but I'm not so sure I'll use him. I'd like to do this on my own.'

Karen shook her head at him. 'Everyone needs help at some time. Don't be so damn proud.'

'I don't like being obliged to anyone.'

'You won't be. You'll be paying him. As Dennis says, he's a fat man, and he charges fat fees.'

Phelan glanced at his wrist and swore softly. 'Can't get out of the habit.'

'Buy yourself another one.'

'I want my own back, and I'm going to get it.' The hard line of Phelan's mouth relaxed into a grin. 'If this man of yours is obsessed with Time maybe he's just the guy to find a missing watch.' He picked up his glass and gazed at what remained of the port. He gained pleasure from colour and had once dabbled in painting. The tawny port was the exact colour of a lion's eyes. For a fleeting moment he had a stab of nostalgia for the continent he loved most. He drained the port. 'I must be going. My body-clock tells me it's past eleven.'

'Have one more,' said Ormerod. 'One for the road while I call a taxi.'

'Thanks, but no. And I think I'll walk. It's about two miles and I could do with the exercise.'

As they moved towards the front door Karen said, 'I'm glad we met up again. It rounds things off somehow. And we must keep in touch.'

'Sure. I hope the American tour goes well.'

'Next time you're in London you must come and stay with us. And if we're out of town, you're welcome to use the house. That's all right, isn't it, Dennis?'

Phelan looked quickly at the other man who smiled, held out his hand, and said, 'Of course. Glad to have met you, Paul.'

Walking back towards Hyde Park Corner, Phelan thought about the evening. In some way, a ghost had been laid. He was glad he was no longer married to Karen, and simply a friend. There had been no awakening of old desires, no longings and no regrets.

Back at the hotel he went straight to bed and was soon asleep.

It was a good sleep, remarkably free from dreams, and when he woke shortly before seven he felt refreshed. Today he would resume his search. The problem was – where should the search begin?

He reached out and switched on the radio. A news broadcast was in progress. He half-listened to an account of a parliamentary fracas which was followed by a report on a demonstration by anti-nuclear protesters. But it was the next item which riveted his attention. He turned up the sound.

The body of a woman found yesterday on the borders of Epping Forest had not yet been identified. Dark-haired and about thirty years of age she was described by the man who found her as being dressed in erotic fashion like a kissogram girl. The cause of her death had not yet been revealed but there was no evidence of sexual interference. The police were anxious to interview a man who had been given a lift by a mini-cab driver near the spot where the body was found and who was dropped off at a bus-stop just outside Epping so that this man could be eliminated from their enquiries.

Phelan switched off the radio. Perhaps Karen had been right and he did need help, but he hated the idea of giving details of his capture and humiliation to a total stranger. As a self-sufficient loner he never asked anyone for help and advice on personal problems. And if he had had the choice of taking on a lion, armed only with a spear, or being psychoanalysed, he would instantly have said, 'Give me the spear.' Not that he expected the man called Samson would psychoanalyse him, but he would want to have every scrap of information about the capture and imprisonment and, in fairness, he would have to be given honest replies, otherwise there was no point in hiring his services.

On the positive side, however, an enquiry agent who could be trusted to keep confidences might be able to find out whether the dead woman was the one who had tried to make him perform like a circus animal. If she was, that was one down and two to go. But also, if she was, there was the mystery to be solved of why her body should have been found near the place where he'd been dumped. Was someone trying to fit him up for murder?

Whether or not the dead woman was his tormentor, he was still determined to find out who was responsible for the plot to abduct and abase him. Common sense told him he would almost certainly need professional help to achieve this aim.

Halfway through the morning he tossed a coin. It came down heads. From his wallet he took out a piece of mauve paper on which Karen had written Samson's address and phone number. Then he picked up the telephone and asked for an outside line.

CHAPTER 5

An hour after his call Phelan was walking down a south London street in which there were snatches of scents from the orient, colour from Africa and the Caribbean, cockney accents and the ancient imperturbability of the Far East. The entrance to Samson's office was sandwiched between a bookmaker's shop and a store which had once sold ironmongery but was now being converted to a mini-supermarket. He climbed a flight of stairs and came to a door where, in gilt lettering, a plaque proclaimed, 'John Samson – Enquiries for Private Enquiries'. Phelan knocked on the door and entered.

A young woman seated behind a word-processor looked up, smiled and said, 'Good morning. Can I help you?'

As she spoke she flicked back a lock of blonde hair from her forehead. She had the sort of looks which at certain angles, and in certain lights, gave her a Scandinavian-type beauty and although she didn't really resemble the Karen of twenty years ago they could have been distant cousins.

'I've got an appointment with Mr Samson,' he said.

'Would you like to take a seat? He's got someone with him at the moment but he won't be long. Can I give you something to read?'

'What have you got?'

She pulled a face. 'Only *The Times* and the *Clockmaker's Gazette*, I'm afraid.'

'I've seen *The Times* so I'll sit this one out, thanks.'

He went to an upright chair which looked as if it had once been at home in a nineteenth-century kitchen.

'When you gave your name,' she said, 'I thought it might be you. I saw the Nan Bellman show. I'm very much on the side of conservation too, but I have doubts about zoos. Luckily some of the worst ones are being closed.'

'I'm glad to hear it.'

'Could I ask you a question?'

'Shoot.'

'Do you find your job attracts hostility, hate mail, that sort of thing?'

'That sort of thing.'

'I guessed as much. When I thought it might be you I tried to figure out why you might need our services. I didn't think it would be connected with Foreign Office diplomatic exchanges. It was more likely to be threats, or something of the sort.' She smiled. 'I shouldn't be saying all this.'

Phelan returned her smile. 'You're a smart lady.'

'I've got a smart boss and I try not to let the side down.' She tapped the word-processor. 'Excuse me, I'd better finish this. It's wanted urgently.'

'Go ahead.'

For about five minutes the silence was broken only by the sound of her fingers on the keys and muted noise from the street below. Then, 'Finished,' she said.

'A busy time of year?' he asked.

She glanced at a calendar on the wall. All the days in September except the thirtieth were crossed out.

'It's picking up,' she said. 'It's usually fairly slack during the summer months. It's after the end of the holiday season and around Christmas that we get a deluge of clients.'

'An interesting job I should think.'

'Yes, but not as interesting as yours.'

They looked at each other in a way that was interested, but an interest not limited to employment.

A party door opened and two men appeared. One was young but looked prematurely withered by some catastrophic tragedy; the other was short-legged and bulky with a big head. Phelan was reminded of a hippopotamus which had made a tilt at his boat down river from Murchison Falls.

Without a sideways look at the receptionist the young man departed. As the door closed she said, 'Mr Phelan to see you.'

The hippo smiled revealing small perfectly white teeth set in an expanse of bright pink gum.

'I'm John Samson. How about a coffee?'

'Thanks, yes.'

'Two coffees, Shandy.'

'Sugar for you, Mr Phelan?' she asked.

'Please.'

'One with sugar and one without,' she said, and gave her boss a challenging look.

'My secretary is diet-conscious,' Samson explained. 'My diet. I can't think why. I'm not overweight, just big-boned. Come along in, Mr Phelan.'

Samson's room might have been the store room of a dealer in antique clocks. None of the movements was working; all had hands frozen at different times. After inviting his client to take a seat, Samson went to a swivel chair behind a desk. Phelan chose a chair near a timepiece which had large roman numerals on its face. In the centre of each numeral, and contained within a small circle, was the arabic equivalent.

In spite of the ubiquitous clocks Phelan was momentarily reminded of being in a bank manager's office. Ever since leaving his father's bank in Freetown early in adult life he had always felt uneasy in banks and, whenever possible, avoided entering them. He felt slightly uneasy here as he waited for Samson to speak.

'My secretary says you might be someone she saw on a chat-show. Was she right?'

'She was.'

'People say television is a time-waster but I don't agree. It may fan prejudices and deaden imagination, but it doesn't waste time. Time can't be wasted. It's Time that wastes us and all our artefacts. Do you agree?'

The Ormerods had warned him that the man was a bit eccentric. In Phelan's opinion most eccentrics were self-indulgent and Samson's waistline confirmed this view, not that it mattered if he did his job well. But digressions on the nature of Time were not getting on with the job and Phelan made this point tersely. He said, 'I'm not interested in Time or television.'

'Well, that's a positive response,' said Samson agreeably. 'Now then, what's the problem?' As he spoke he leaned forward clasping his hands in front of him. An encouraging smile made him look more like a friendly Buddha than a pachyderm.

'My problem,' said Phelan, 'is a missing watch. I want you to find it.'

As he had hoped, the corpulent detective lost his smile and eyes that had been half-closed under heavy lids opened wide.

'You want me to find your watch? Your wrist-watch?'

'That's right.'

Samson sat back as if to reappraise his client. 'I've had dozens of cases involving missing persons but never one concerning a missing watch.'

'Besides the watch I want you to find the person or three persons who took it.'

Samson lowered an arm and, unseen by Phelan, switched on a tape recorder.

'You know who these persons are and you wish me to go to them and reclaim your watch?'

'I don't know who they are.'

'I see. So up to three people you don't know have taken your wrist-watch. Was it taken in lieu of payment for some service? Did you, for example, overlook payment to a dealer in arms and ammunition?'

Phelan shook his head. 'It was nothing like that.' The man sitting on the other side of the room didn't inspire confidence; in fact, he didn't inspire anything except antipathy. The thought of recounting a mortifying experience to him was almost intolerable. But a coin had been tossed and it had come down heads. He pressed on. 'This is going to sound incredible,' he said.

'I've heard quite a few incredible things, and let me assure you, if you need assurance, that none goes further than this office.'

'It had better not.'

'It won't. I promise you.'

Phelan took a deep breath, squared his shoulders, and started with an account of how he had picked up Cindy, or been picked up by her. He told of the television interview, of how he had declined an invitation to the hospitality room and left the building with Cindy hoping to find a taxi, of how his pocket had been picked, of the pursuit, of how someone in the middle of a crowded pavement had managed to inject him with a knock-out drug.

At this point Shandy entered with two cups of coffee. 'I'm sorry I've been so long,' she said, 'but the phone hasn't stopped ringing and, when it did, I couldn't remember where I'd hidden the sugar.' She placed a cup in front of Samson. 'Without,' she said. Then she brought the other cup to Phelan.

'With?' he asked.

'With,' she replied and as she spoke she changed the cup from right to left hand, and as she gave it to him she raised the third finger of her left hand very slightly so that he could see a wedding ring.

He took the cup. 'Noted,' he said.

When she had left the room Samson opened a desk drawer, took out two lumps of sugar and dropped them into his coffee. He stirred it with a silver paper knife.

'You were saying, Mr Phelan, that you'd been injected with some drug.'

This was the most difficult part. All men were enemies unless they proved themselves otherwise. Samson hadn't yet proved himself. Phelan forced himself to continue. 'The drug knocked me out.'

'Yes, so you've already said. But evidently you recovered. Where and when?'

'I don't know where and, since my watch had been taken, I don't know when. But I was alone, in a cage, in a basement or cellar.' He paused and almost inaudibly added, 'All my clothes had been taken as well as my watch.'

He gave Samson a piercing look. If the fat detective had given the glimmer of a smile Phelan would have walked out. But Samson remained impassive as a sleeping hippopotamus. Phelan proceeded with his narrative. He told of how he'd been visited by three hooded women who had stared at him and then gone away, walking slowly up the stairs. He had noticed that one woman had a ring on every finger.

'How did you know they were women?' Samson interjected.

'Height, but not height alone. There was a difference in hip width. Women have wider hips than men. And their hands weren't men's hands. Anyway, one of them spoke through a cavity near the top of the stairs. She told me I'd been tranquillised in the same way as the animals I trap.'

'With a lesser dose presumably,' said Samson, 'otherwise it could be lethal.'

'Right.'

'So someone knows a lot about drugs. Go on, please.'

Phelan told him of the whisky. 'The bottle had already been opened. I was thirsty. Dehydrated. I drank. I should have known better. In the tropics you're a fool if you drink alcohol to

46

quench thirst. It tasted like it looked, Glenfiddich malt, but it had a mule's kick. I think it may have been laced with pure alcohol. I began to feel really drunk, and then they came back. But this time one of them was dressed in a fantasy outfit and she had a vicious-looking whip.'

The lids were low over Samson's eyes as he said, 'Was she the one with rings?'

'No.'

'Carry on, please.'

This was the hardest part. 'I was told I had to perform like a circus animal,' said Phelan bitterly.

'I can see that inflicting such an indignity might give them vicarious pleasure,' said Samson, 'but surely there was more to it than that?'

'They wanted me to sign a statement publicly renouncing my trade.'

'What happened next?'

Phelan told of the futile attempt to mount the Elsan in the hope of using it as a platform to jump from, and how he had toppled the masked woman but been tranquillised a second time. 'When I came to I was in a small clearing in what I now know was Epping Forest.'

'Still naked?'

'Yes, but my clothes were beside me. Everything was there. Wallet, passport, everything except my watch. I made my way to a road, hitched a lift and next morning got back to London.'

'And your watch is so valuable you want to employ me to recover it. What's its make?'

'Rolex oyster, but I want you to find the women too.'

'So that you can take legal action for unlawful detention and criminal assault?'

'You find them. I'll decide how to deal with them.'

'Why me?' asked Samson. 'Why me out of all the agencies in London?'

'Personal recommendation. Mr and Mrs Ormerod.'

'Ormerod?' Samson closed his eyes to blot out visual distraction while he concentrated on recollection. 'I remember. Marseilles. How are they?'

'Fine.' Phelan paused. 'There is one other thing. A woman's body was found yesterday and it looks as if it was near the spot where I was dumped.'

'Yes, I've read about it.'

'She was dressed like the woman who tried to make me crawl.'

'I realise that.' Samson finished his coffee and pushed the cup away. 'When you told me you'd recovered consciousness somewhere near Epping I made the connection. And more than a coincidence, I'd think. You're in trouble.'

'Someone trying to fit me up?'

'Why should anyone want to do that?'

Samson's question was gently spoken, almost coaxing in tone, and Phelan sensed something lay behind the innocuous enquiry. 'I don't know why anyone should want to fix me,' he said. 'I don't think even an animal rights crank would try to pin a murder on me.'

'Oh, it was a murder was it? The report I read said the cause of death hadn't been established.'

'I assume it was murder.'

'You assume it was murder,' Samson repeated, and now his voice had a derisive edge.

'Yes, I do. How do you think she died? Accidentally?'

Samson gave a short laugh. 'I doubt if it was an accident, but it might have been an unwitting act of homicide.'

'What do you mean by that?'

'What do you think I mean?'

Phelan began to feel angry. He hadn't come to a down-market area of London to play word games with a fat clock-freak. 'I don't know what the hell you mean,' he said.

'I mean the woman's death might have been caused by someone unaware of what he was doing. . . . Can you be sure you didn't kill her?'

For a moment Phelan saw Samson as the deadliest of enemies, a second Verhaeren, but he managed to control his rising anger. 'You'd better explain what you mean by that.'

'There are recorded instances of people who have killed while under the influence of alcohol who genuinely didn't remember what they'd done, and alcohol is only one drug. Minds have been bent beyond recall by LSD and other hallucinogenic drugs. Apart from that, there are cases of people who have killed in their sleep. In 1961, for instance, an American soldier stationed in England, a veteran of the Korean war, was acquitted of a murder he committed in his sleep.'

48

Phelan looked hard at the man sitting behind the desk and knew it was a mistake to dismiss him as a fat clock-freak. 'Let's get this straight,' he said. 'I didn't do it.'

'You don't think you did, but you must admit that, as I've said, you're in trouble.'

'I don't admit anything.'

'You came to me asking me to find a missing wrist-watch. I'll try to do that, and to find whoever took it. But it could serve you better if I tried to find out who killed the woman who is almost certainly the same woman who got into the cage with you.'

Phelan said, 'It had occurred to me someone was trying to frame me, but not that anyone could think I'd done it.' He picked up his cup and drank.

'Like something stronger?' asked Samson. 'A whisky perhaps, or are you off whisky?'

'I wouldn't say no to a whisky.'

Samson got up and ambled to a small cabinet. He produced a bottle and two glasses. 'I'll join you,' he said. 'My calorie-conscious secretary won't approve, but I don't mind. I'm not an approval-seeker.' While he poured he went on, 'I once had a client who needed everything he did to be approved by his wife. He couldn't move without her approval. At least, that was her story when I found her. She'd run away from a man who was really an insecure child.' He handed Phelan a whisky. 'Cheers.'

'Good luck.'

Samson laughed. 'That's a toast worth having. I've never met anyone in my line of business who doesn't believe in luck. Napoleon thought a man shouldn't be made a general unless he was lucky and Churchill said you should always choose people who were lucky as your friends, and who am I to argue with Napoleon or Churchill?'

Phelan stretched his mouth into the semblance of a smile; it looked more like a pained grimace. He was hiring a detective, not a source for a dictionary of quotations. 'Where will you start?' he asked.

'I don't usually discuss that with clients,' said Samson, 'but in your case I'll make an exception. As a first step I shall want the fullest possible description of this Cindy, and as much as you can tell me about the three women, and I shall also need to know the exact place where you were abducted and where you were

49

abandoned. I shall find out about animal rights groups and their extreme fringes. ... You did tell me the woman with the whip said, "I'm expert at this treatment"?'

'Yes.'

'I shall put out feelers in the murky underworld of aberrant sex which some dignify with the word "sub-culture", and that's all I'm telling you except that I'm not cheap. I charge well above the going rate for enquiry agents.'

'What is the tariff?'

'One hundred pounds a day plus expenses. Money can always make things move fast and that's one reason why my fees are high.'

'At that price you'd better come up with results.'

'I shall, Mr Phelan. I shall.'

During the next hour Phelan was exhaustively questioned so that by the end of the interview Samson knew everything that could be recollected. When it was finished Phelan said, 'Don't bother to show me out. I know the way.'

They shook hands. 'I'll be in touch,' said Samson.

As he passed through the outer office Phelan paused by Shandy and said, 'If you weren't married I'd ask if you were doing anything tonight.'

'If I wasn't married,' she replied, 'I'd tell you I was free tonight.'

CHAPTER 6

The mini-cab driver, Daryll Stubbs, had heard the news of a body being found on the border of Epping Forest on his car radio. The police were appealing for help from anyone in the vicinity who might have seen anything suspicious during the night. When he got home he told his wife about the man who'd thumbed a lift from him. 'A right rude sod,' he concluded.

'You must go to the police,' she said.

'I don't want to get involved.'

'You go. It's your duty.'

'They might keep me hours. I could lose business.'

'You go,' she said. 'He insulted us and our unborn, and besides, like I say, it's your duty.'

An hour later he was poring over a large-scale map spread across a table in a police incident room watched by two plain-clothes detectives. After a great deal of thought he pointed to a place by a road and said, 'It was just about there.'

One of the detectives marked the spot in pencil. It was close to a place ringed by a red circle. 'Not more than six hundred yards away, I'd say,' he remarked to his colleague as he put down the pencil.

The other man, Detective Inspector Cook, picked up the pencil and began twirling it between his fingers. He had the features of someone whose facial muscles have hardened and become almost immovable through seeing too many maimed bodies and hearing too many cries of despair. He took up the questioning.

'You say this man told you he'd abandoned his car, a Saab, but he didn't say what was wrong with the car?'

'He just said the engine had cut. I thought he might have run out of petrol like. I told him it had happened once to me when I was out with a girl and she'd got hold of the wrong end of my stick, if you know what I mean.'

Although Cook's face remained impassive his mouth gave a slight twitch. 'She got hold of the wrong end of your stick, did she?'

The other detective smiled more broadly. Detective Sergeant Wilkins had been on many cases with Cook and although he didn't think much of Cook's sense of humour which usually involved heavily accented puns he knew when to appear amused. And you needed humour in this job, and smutty humour kept things firmly on earth. You couldn't get downhearted if there were jokes about girls getting hold of a man's stick.

'How did he get hold of the wrong end of the stick?' Cook asked.

'He was bloody rude, wasn't he?'

'In what way?'

Daryll Stubbs shifted uncomfortably on a metal alloy chair. 'Well, when I told him the confrontation with my bird had a happy ending, we got married and was expecting like, he asked what was happy about that, sort of sneering.'

Cook weighed the information. Sometimes the most irrelevant detail provided a lead. 'Could it be,' he asked, 'that he was being deliberately rude to stop any further talk? Did you get the impression he wanted to say as little as possible?'

'Yeah, yeah. I did get that impression.'

Cook continued twirling the pencil, using his fingers to turn it round and round, manipulating it with the dexterity of a conjuror. In his spare time he enjoyed performing tricks at children's parties: more than anything else he found that by occupying his hands his powers of concentration were increased.

'When this chap spoke did you notice anything about his accent? Was it a north country one, for instance?'

Stubbs frowned in an effort of recollection. 'No, not north country.'

'Was he what's known as well-spoken?'

'Yes, well no, not exactly. He sounded English. I mean, he wasn't a foreigner, but then again, not exactly English.'

'Australian? South African?'

'No. A bit South African maybe.'

'Rather clipped speech?'

'Yeah, sort of.'

'And he didn't tell you anything except the car was a Saab and it had broken down?'

'That's right. I told him I'd never driven a Saab. I asked if it had fuel injection.'

'And what did he say?'

'Well, for a moment I thought he wasn't going to say nothing but then he said it was. I got the feeling he didn't know that much about cars with fuel injection.'

'Now, Mr Stubbs, I'd like you to think very carefully. We'd like as full a description as you can give of this man. How tall do you reckon he was?'

'Oh, a six-footer at least.'

'You sound sure.'

'I am. Tall men never find it that easy to get into my cab. They have to crouch.'

'How old? Approximately.'

Stubbs rubbed his forehead as if to wipe out a frown that had become stuck. 'That's hard. It was dark.'

'But the light came on when the door was opened?'

'Oh, yeah, but I didn't get more than a glimpse.'

'Between twenty and thirty?'

'More than that. Between forty and fifty I'd say, and nearer fifty than forty.'

'White, black, mixed race?'

'White, but tanned. He looked as if he'd just come back from a month on the Costa del Sol.'

'Colour of hair?'

'I can't honestly say.'

'Plenty of it?'

'I don't remember. He wasn't bald.'

'Anything special about his face? Big nose? Moustache? Strong jaw?'

'I can't honestly remember. I didn't look at him all that much. I had to keep my eyes on the road. But I don't think he had a tache.'

'How was he dressed? What was he wearing?'

A look of relief came to Stubbs's face. 'That I do remember. It was a safari suit. Very nice. Hard to tell the colour but it looked a pale blue. I've thought about it since. Wouldn't mind one like that for myself next time I take the missus to Spain.'

'What else can you remember about this man?'

The pencil rotated as if caught in perpetual motion.

'Nothing.'

'What else did you talk about before the conversation dried up?'

'I can't remember nothing.'

'You told us you dropped him off at the bus-stop by Corton Road. Did he ask you to do that?'

'No. He asked me to drop him by a phone box. But I was cheesed off with him and told him there was a box down the road.' Stubbs hesitated. 'To give him credit he did offer to pay for the lift but I didn't want nothing from him. He'd got my goat by his nasty manner.'

'What else can you remember?'

'I don't remember nothing else. . . . Oh yes, just after he'd got in he went through his pockets as if he was looking for something. I asked if he'd lost anything and he said "No." But I think – well, this is just a guess – I think he'd lost his watch because he had to lean forward to see the time on the car's clock. The dashboard isn't all that well lit.' Hurriedly, in case bad lighting constituted an offence, he went on, 'It's just the clock. The other instruments are fine. Very well lit.'

The pencil was still. The moment Cook heard that a watch might be missing he had stopped twirling it.

'I think that's all, Mr Stubbs. I'd like to thank you for being so public-spirited in coming forward in response to our appeal.'

'That's all right. Being a law-abiding man myself I like to help the police.'

'I wish there were more like you,' replied Cook with feeling. 'I'm glad to hear you say it. And I'm sure in the spirit of co-operation, although you found it difficult to see the man in question, you'll spare us a little more time.'

Apprehension clouded Stubbs's features. 'What do you want? I've told you all I know.'

'And very useful it's been. But we'd like to have a shot at building up a Photofit picture.'

'But like I said, I only got a glimpse. I don't want no identity parade.'

'You might surprise yourself how much you do remember, Mr Stubbs. Memory is like a computer bank; tap the right keys and you unlock its secrets. Chance plays a part, as hackers well

54

know. By different methods, hypnotists can find the key. Come and give it a try.'

'OK, but like I say, it was dark in the cab.'

But Daryll Stubbs was no hacker, and Detective Inspector Cook no hypnotist, and the result of trying to assemble a Photofit picture was disappointing. However, Cook was not too downcast. A vital fact had been revealed and when Stubbs had gone he turned to his junior.

'You got the bit about him looking at the time on the car clock?'

'Yes. It'll be interesting to see what Forensic come up with.'

'I don't expect a lot,' said Cook. 'A Rolex oyster isn't uncommon. But the strap might be helpful. It looked like crocodile but it might be something different. . . . So he's tall, tanned, and speaks in a way which could be colonial. He has a safari suit and may be minus a watch.' He sighed. 'It's a start.'

'It's not bad, and we might get other public-spirited helpers.'

Both men chuckled as if a joke had been cracked.

'Still no record of an abandoned Saab?' Cook asked. 'Every local recovery service has been questioned?'

'Every one, and no record at all.'

'AA? RAC?'

'No record.'

'If there wasn't transport of some sort, how did he get there? And how did he get the body there?'

Wilkins grinned and looked at the pencil which was again being twirled between agile fingers. 'By magic, maybe. Maybe the Super was on to a good thing when he put you on this case.'

CHAPTER 7

The dead woman was identified as Maxine Eastbank, a thirty-one-year-old former air hostess, who had for the past three years followed the more lucrative occupation of professional dominatrix. She had owned and lived in a well-furnished Victorian villa which fronted a road in Stamford Hill, north London. A railway cutting lay on the opposite side of the road but double glazing of windows had ensured that she wasn't disturbed by trains. She had employed a maid whose duty was to show a client into a private room if he was early for an appointment. Here he could help himself to drinks and read a scatter of glossy top-class magazines; or he could sit and admire erotic Japanese shunga paintings which adorned one wall or gaze at another wall where an oil painting depicted a nude male kneeling before a woman wearing Edwardian dress. She was in the act of lifting up a voluminous skirt.

The comfort of this room with its deep plush armchairs and walnut side-tables was in complete contrast to a basement below which was fitted out as a torture chamber. To reach this chamber clients had to pass a door marked 'Private'. Behind the door was a small room which contained sound equipment and cameras and from a panel set in the wall it was possible to view events taking place in the chamber. Most clients during their torture assumed that the gap in the wall at the top of the stairs was connected to an air vent; only the most privileged ones, for a substantial payment, were permitted to watch the sufferings of fellow victims from this room.

At an autopsy a Home Office pathologist ascertained that the cause of death was a subdural haemorrhage resulting from a blow to the head which might not have been fatal but for an abnormally thin skull and dura. It was impossible to tell what sort of weapon had been used to strike the blow but from the star-shaped wound it was thought to be a blunt or rounded instrument. It was estimated that approximately twelve hours had passed between death and the time the corpse was found.

Detectives interviewed the maid who was a young out-of-work actress who had only been in the job a fortnight and was thinking of quitting employment which she was finding uncongenial. 'Not that I'm a prude,' she had said. 'If grown men want to play kinky games, let them get on with it but I object to having to tell them to shove off and come at the proper time if there's already a client in the waiting room. There are some,' she explained, 'who get quite turned on by being ordered to wait and they deliberately come early; but they look so silly and it makes me feel embarrassed.'

For three days before the death of her mistress she had been instructed not to come to the house as her services weren't required for the next few days. She had no idea why she had been laid off on full pay but thought perhaps Ms Eastbank was going on a short holiday.

The house was searched. A red leather-bound book was discovered inside a drawer in the principal bedroom; it contained names and addresses of various clients with coded notes on their chosen treatment. The men whose names appeared in the book were discreetly contacted by the police and asked to come for questioning. They were strongly advised to comply with this request so that they could be ruled out of the enquiries.

A series of interviews took place. Some men sheepishly admitted that they knew 'the lady in question' and begged that their wives should be kept in ignorance of their shameful peccadilloes. Others tried to bluster and bluff it out by denying all knowledge of Maxine Eastbank. One man said that his visits to the house of correction were for the purpose of psychotherapy and another said that for him a whipping by his dominatrix was akin to a religious experience and he quoted extensively from the literature on flagellation citing the lives and works of the early Christian fathers.

Some had alibis for the evening in question; some had not; it was evident that this line of investigation would take time. Fairly sure that the murderer would recently have lost a watch and be one of the men he called 'punters', Detective Inspector Cook took part in most of the interviews.

He had ordered the clock to be removed from the room and at

some time during the questioning he would glance at his wrist and say, 'My watch is slow, have you got the right time?' The punter would look at his own watch and Cook would pass some comment aimed at finding out whether it was a new watch. One man said, 'This is my spare. I lost my other one. I think it must have dropped off somewhere.' In a casual voice Cook asked, 'Was it a good one? What make was it?' To his disappointment the man replied, 'It only cost ten quid but it was a quartz and it kept perfect time.'

The Rolex oyster wasn't a quartz watch and would have cost very much more.

If, in reply to the query about the time, a man said, 'I don't wear a watch,' Cook would ferret out whether a watch was never worn or one had been lost and not yet been replaced. But as suspects came and went, some to have alibis checked, others to be temporarily ruled out of the reckoning, he began to wonder if he'd ever find a man who'd lost a Rolex oyster on a crocodile leather strap.

After days of interviewing men whose responses ranged from the pathetically nervous to the aggressively defiant Cook had reached only one firm conclusion. All of Maxine Eastbank's clients belonged to a higher earning bracket than he. They included a highly paid industrialist, a public school headmaster, an under-secretary in the Civil Service, as well as a sprinkling drawn from banking, accountancy, the law and politics. 'If you put all that lot together,' remarked Cook when reporting to a detective chief superintendent, 'you'd have enough talent to form a cabinet and run the bloody country.'

While he was interviewing men named in the address book other detectives were questioning known prostitutes who specialised in domination but none of them was forthcoming with useful information although it was learned that Maxine Eastbank was generally disliked by those who knew her. Nobody could throw light on her private life, which she had kept very private, but it was thought she had lesbian tendencies.

She had a middle-class background and her parents lived in Tonbridge. They had not seen their daughter for two years and had been horrified by her murder: they had been unaware of the nature of her profession and had no idea who might be responsible for her death.

While Cook was patiently pursuing his formal investigation

Samson was amassing information on animal rights activists but drawing blank responses whenever he mentioned the name of Maxine Eastbank in connection with trapped animals. Unlike some enquiry agents Samson did his best to keep on good terms with the police. Early in his career an elderly lawyer had advised him to help the police whenever he could, not to trespass on their territory, and to contribute regularly and generously to the Police Benevolent Fund. On the whole Samson had followed this advice and he had contacts with the local police and in New Scotland Yard but he knew that if he tried to get information on Maxine Eastbank it would arouse curiosity and even a rookie detective might guess he could be representing someone with a vested interest. Until Phelan could be proved innocent Samson decided it would be wise not to contact the police.

The murder attracted some media attention and the life-style of Maxine Eastbank received titillating coverage masquerading as serious reportage. Samson scanned the newspapers but couldn't find any reference to a sideline in animal rights activities or any indication that the dead woman had an alternative interest to that of making money from her profession. The law of libel prevented her clients being named although rumours were rife that a Member of Parliament was involved and *Private Eye* had some harmful fun at his expense.

But it wasn't long before the murder, and details of Maxine Eastbank's profession, became stale copy, swept out of sight by the hijacking of a Boeing 747 and a bloody military coup in West Africa. Phelan, tired of being pestered by people who loathed his trade, moved to a hotel near Piccadilly Circus. Here, in the Eros bar one lunchtime, he met Samson by appointment. They went to a corner table after ordering drinks. Samson, ever conscious of personal comfort, sat on a green draylon-covered settee while Phelan took a chair opposite him.

Without any preliminaries Phelan said, 'Let's see it then.'

Samson unzipped a briefcase and produced a gloss photograph. It was a head and shoulders portrait of Maxine Eastbank which he had obtained from a friend in Fleet Street.

'Is this the woman with the whip?'

After examining the photo carefully, at first closely and then at arm's length, Phelan handed it back.

'I can't say. I was more concerned with watching her whip-hand than her face, and her nose and eyes were covered by a mask. The mouth could be similar but the hair style is quite different. Hers was short. In the photo it's long.'

'She may have changed her style after the photo was taken. It's not a recent one.'

Samson put away the photo and zipped up his briefcase.

'Have you got anywhere yet?' Phelan asked.

'You told me you were near the Post Office on Shepherd's Road, right by the common, when you were attacked. The time was about eight fifteen and there was a crowd of people around.'

'That's right.'

'I've been there twice at that time. The Post Office was closed and hardly any pedestrians were around. There were some kids on the common, dogs being walked, but not much else. I think the crowd, or throng, who closed in on you was organised. A group, possibly an animal rights group, was probably involved.'

Phelan nodded. 'Anything else?'

'I'm checking out the known organisations in the animal welfare field and, believe me, there are more than you'd think. And some of the larger ones have splinter groups. I'm having to tread cautiously. Most people I've spoken to are very pro-animal but are careful to stress this doesn't mean they are anti-human. But I'm persisting. There's quite a way to go on this line of enquiry.'

'Good.'

'I'd like to know what line the police are following,' Samson continued. 'I'm fairly sure they'll be interviewing the lady's clients and maybe some other women in the same type of business. The obvious motive for a murder would be a client who might have been threatened with blackmail or hated her for bringing out a facet of himself which he hated.' Samson smiled. 'That sounds like a psychological angle but we detectives have to be amateur psychologists.'

Rather grimly Phelan returned the smile. 'I've never been much good at that.' With a touch of mordant humour he added, 'People who go to be psychoanalysed need their heads tested.'

'I won't argue with that.' Samson finished his drink and glanced towards the bar. 'Would you like another?'

'No, thanks. I'm off to pick up some keys. I'm changing my address again, going somewhere more private. I'm too accessible here.' He paused. 'I've already been tracked down here and abusive letters and calls from anonymous ill-wishers have started up again. I'm not the most popular man in town and some individuals want to hound me out, or better still, to drop dead.'

'You'd better let me have the new address. Where are you going?'

'My ex-wife offered the use of their place before she left for America. A woman comes in each day for a short while to clean and check through but apart from her I shall be on my own and I prefer being on my own to' – Phelan motioned with his arm towards other tables where hotel guests and visitors were drinking – 'being in a place like this.'

'No plans to return to Africa?'

'Not yet.' He looked Samson straight in the eyes. 'I'd be telling a lie if I said I hadn't been thinking about what you told me. People killing under the influence of drugs, or even in their sleep. I want to know I'm clear on that score. But much more, I don't want to leave until I've squared the account with those three bitches. Some men aren't the sort to carry a grudge. I'm not like that.'

Samson sighed. 'Desire for revenge or retribution seems as old as mankind. An eye for an eye. Nemesis . . . You'd better let me have that address.'

Phelan took out a pen and, using the hotel's wine list which stood on the table, he scribbled an address and a telephone number. 'What's your next move?' he asked.

'I shall carry on investigating animal rights groups but also I shall do something the police are almost certainly doing. I shall take soundings from contacts who represent the oldest profession. I may find out more about Maxine Eastbank and the woman who introduced herself to you as Cindy.'

In the cool, air-conditioned foyer they shook hands and Samson said, 'I'll be in touch.'

As he passed through swing doors he was brushed by a gust of warm air from the street. Physically lazy, he never walked if a taxi was available, but London was enjoying an unexpected spell of Indian summer and, in Piccadilly, taxis were stuck like black flies in jam. He decided to walk to his next destination even though it meant weaving his bulk around idle sightseers, linked-arms lovers, lunchtime office workers, darting children and late season tourist parties.

He was sweating by the time he turned off Piccadilly to enter the peaceful enclave of Shepherd Market. He picked his way through drifts of people to a mews flat occupied by a woman who had been one of his first clients and who sent him a card and a bottle of brandy at Christmas every year.

Vanessa Vincent, now almost fifty, was well enough off to entertain only selected clients, but she had come to Samson in the days when she was a street-walker. He had never forgotten her opening words – 'I've got an identity crisis.'

She had continued by explaining that at the age of three she had been adopted and knew nothing of her own parentage except that her father had been a sailor who had deserted her mother whose name was Bette Hansen. She had a yearning to find and be reunited with her mother. Could Samson help? He could and did. The mother had since died but Vanessa had never forgotten the man who had helped her and, apart from the Christmas gift, she had also sent two or three clients his way.

A maid opened the door and showed him into a lounge which had *art nouveau* ornaments on the mantel of a marble fireplace. A huge brass eagle on a plinth looked as if it was about to fly out of the folds of orange velvet curtains. There was a restlessness about the room which was reinforced by the nervous vitality of the woman who hurried forward to greet Samson with a 'Darling!' and then her left cheek and then her right cheek, and then, 'How lovely to see you.'

He was engulfed in a waft of expensive scent.

The maid brought iced drinks and canapés of smoked salmon and caviare. Samson's eyes lit up.

'I thought you might like a snack,' said Vanessa.

'You know me well.'

'Actually, I don't. I've known many men well, but not you. I sometimes think you missed your true vocation. You should have been a priest. Roman Catholic, of course, and celibate.'

Samson laughed and took another canapé.

'It's true, darling. You must have heard hundreds of confessions and, in your funny old way, given absolution when you can.'

'I'm an agnostic who wonders about dualism.'

'I know, I know. But you are priest material.'

'I don't come today as a priest, but a supplicant.'

Vanessa Vincent had a small, unremarkable face: her beauty and attraction was in big, luminous, violet eyes. She turned the full force of these eyes on Samson. 'A supplicant, eh? Well, that gives me an edge. What are you supplicating for?' Her eyes shone. 'Me?' she teased.

'If only I could say "Yes" to that, but I can't. This is a less worthy petition.'

'In the course of business, I imagine.'

'It is. Do you know anything about Maxine Eastbank, the woman whose body was found in Epping Forest?'

'I know of her. But her scene and mine are quite different. I've never been into the heavy S-M stuff. . . . Have you got a client who was in her clutches? Poor devil. Is the finger on him?'

'Not yet, but he could be. He was never a paying customer, but a woman who had the same technique as Miss Eastbank did have him in her clutches, against his will, for a couple of days and he's suffering from a bad attack of loss of dignity and wants retribution.' Samson opened his briefcase and took out the photograph. 'I've shown him this but he can't be sure whether or not she was the woman.'

'I don't understand. Surely he can identify her from that photo.'

'He never really saw her. She wore a mask and the hair style was different.'

'I see.' Vanessa Vincent sipped her drink and as she raised her glass a diamond ring, the gift of a Venezuelan horse-breeder, flashed a blue light from her finger. 'You're wondering if I have any idea who the woman might be, if it's not Eastbank?'

'Yes.'

She put down her glass. 'The short answer, darling, is No. Of course, I do know one or two who specialise in the kinky stuff. There's one who lives not a hundred miles from here.'

'I think I may know her,' said Samson, 'but this one lived in Stamford Hill – if it is Eastbank – and she had a sort of torture chamber.'

'That's par for the course. You aren't a top-class dom unless you've got your own custom-made dungeon. Incidentally, did you know that Eastbank was known as the Man-Tamer, Maxine the Man-Tamer?'

'I read that in one of the papers,' said Samson.

'They rather like these nicknames. There's a Whipping Wanda and a Stinging Sally. You don't have to be psychic to guess what they cater for.'

'What is man-taming?'

'Oh, that's the whole gamut, not just CP. Bondage,

humiliation gearing, everything.' She put her hand to her mouth as though she'd suddenly had a second thought. 'Wait a minute. I might be able to help. There's a young man who's researching the subject. An earnest-looking boy after a PhD. Genuine, as far as I could tell. Not a sensation seeker. He's interviewed hundreds of girls and as my name came up from time to time he asked to see me. I couldn't tell him anything he didn't already know and since my scene isn't *that* scene he didn't stay long.' She stood up and went to an escritoire. 'I've got a note of his address somewhere. He should be able to tell you about the Man-Tamer. If anyone can fill you in on her, he should be able to.'

'Would he know if she had any other activities, apart from professional ones?'

'I'm sure he would.' She produced a slip of paper. 'Ah, here it is. Simon Jones. I should warn you he seems rather left-wing. He thinks capitalism and prostitution go together, particularly high-powered capitalism and dominant prostitutes. He called it a necessary paradox, whatever that might mean.'

Samson took the paper from her. 'Does the name Cindy mean anything to you?'

'Should it?'

'I think she was on the game and she was with him when he got snatched.'

'Snatched?' She sounded incredulous.

'He was drugged and woke up in captivity.'

'How absolutely bizarre. Tell me more.'

'I'd rather not. You don't know of a Cindy?'

'I don't know every little scrubber,' replied Vanessa Vincent haughtily.

'I had to ask.'

She relaxed. 'Yes. All in the line of duty. Where does this Cindy operate? What's her patch?'

'He can't remember the name of the bar where he met her in Soho but reckons he could find it again.'

'A prostitute in Soho,' she said with mock surprise. 'You astonish me.'

'She occupied a flat in Shepherd's Bush but when he tried to find it he drew a blank.'

'Sounds like a put-up blackmail job. What's so special about this man?'

64

'Forgive me, Vanessa . . .'

'But your lips are sealed. Confidentiality is the name of the game. I understand. And I'll put out feelers about fem/doms and Cindy and I'll let you know if I have any luck.'

'I shouldn't want our wonderful police . . .'

'I'll be the soul of discretion, darling.'

Because their friendship had been long-standing Samson didn't leave as soon as he'd found out all he could. He had another drink and some more canapés, and listened to a colourful account of her adventures since their last meeting. He was glad he was a friend and not a lover. One of her tricks, and it was the trick of all high-class prostitutes she admitted, was to keep lovers in suspense, and Samson didn't like being kept in suspense.

Back in his office he gazed fondly at Shandy. She was a woman who didn't muck around. She said what she thought and didn't keep you waiting on tenterhooks. There was no equivocation. No suspense nonsense. You knew where you stood with Shandy.

She was busy on the word-processor.

'Anything happen while I was out?' he asked.

'Yes. I've got some news for you.'

'What?'

'Can't tell you now. Wait till I've finished this.'

'To hell with that. What news?'

She stopped working. 'What's got into you?'

'Nothing. It may have escaped your notice, but I employ you. You don't employ me. What news?'

'Heavens, we are touchy this afternoon.'

He came towards her and leaned over the word-processor. 'Do you like keeping men in suspense?'

'What a question to ask! No, of course I don't.' She thought for a moment. 'Unless, that is, I want to entice them. Does that answer it?'

'Perfectly,' he said, moving towards his room.

'Don't go. It's good news. The flat over the road, the one you were after, is on the market again. Shall I get the estate agents for you?'

Suddenly, inexplicably, Samson felt very weary. 'I'll take it in my room,' he said.

Why was it, he wondered, that whenever he had a case where sex raised its hundred hideous hydra-heads he wished Fate had destined him to be a lighthouse keeper, or a Trappist monk, or a troglodyte, instead of a humble private eye.

CHAPTER 8

After an inquest, at which a verdict of murder by some person or persons unknown was returned, Maxine Eastbank was buried according to the rites of the Church of England. Cook and another detective, wearing dark lounge suits, stood on the fringe of a small crowd of mourners.

It was a gathering of incompatibles. Parents and elderly relatives kept a tensely narrow distance from two women who, in spite of the warm weather, were wearing thigh-length boots. A bearded Jew in black from Stamford Hill's predominantly Hasidic community had come motivated by a spirit of charity, and a Jamaican cab-driver, who had often been hired by the dead woman, was there as a mark of respect to a customer whose tips had always been generous. Former clients were conspicuously absent and from the police viewpoint it was a wasted morning, or as Cook expressed it, with a laboured emphasis on the pun, 'a wasted mourning'.

Other aspects of the enquiry were less wasteful. Under interrogation a bank manager broke down and unexpectedly confessed to embezzlement of bank monies to pay for his visits, and a prostitute gave evidence which was to lead to the smashing of a vice ring. But little progress was made towards the goal of finding a killer except that the process of elimination left a handful of men who were unable to account convincingly for their activities on the night of the murder.

But Cook persisted. From experience he knew that if one persisted with single-minded application for long enough a lucky break must come. The skill lay in recognising the break when it appeared. Unlike some police officers, he shared work problems with his wife, a schoolmistress who taught at a comprehensive school. He respected her intuitions. More than once she had illuminated shadowy uncertainties with a flash of insight.

One night, after they had gone to bed, she said, 'I don't think she was killed because she was blackmailing someone, I think she'd just gone too far.'

'What do you mean, love?' he asked.

'Well, anyone who pushes someone too far could get a wrong reaction. It's like a people's revolution against a dictatorship.'

'You mean – counter-productive.' Cook spoke the word in a slow, rounded way, as if savouring a new favourite in his vocabulary.

She yawned. 'I'm sleepy.' Moments later she was asleep, but he stayed awake for a long time.

In every interview he had asked, 'Did she never exceed the limits of your endurance?' but the question had stemmed from natural curiosity rather than professional probing. He wished now he had pressed the question hard, and rigorously explored the answers, instead of accepting whatever reply was given.

Most answers had been given in a subdued voice by men whose eyes were lowered in embarrassment. These were invariably on the lines of, 'She knew exactly how much I could take and when to stop.' It seemed that Maxine Eastbank had developed to a fine art the technique of bringing pain and pleasure to an optimum, but not unbearable, pitch. And because it seemed only common sense for her to pay regard to a man's limits of tolerance, otherwise she'd soon have no clients, Cook had been satisfied with the answers.

Nevertheless, he still thought the watch was the best lead to the murderer; the killer's motivation could be discovered once the watch fitted the correct wrist. Although it had proved impossible to find out when and where the watch had been acquired, expert analysis had revealed that the strap was made from the hide of an African crocodile and was many years old. Further, the buckle which fastened it was larger than normal and made of inferior Egyptian gold. The watch had therefore almost certainly been purchased in Africa and this fact, together with Stubbs's recollection of his passenger's accent, pointed to someone who might be on a visit to England.

All the men named in Maxine Eastbank's red book were resident in England.

Another aspect of the case which puzzled Cook was why the maid should have been sent away for a few days. Nobody had seen Maxine Eastbank from the time the maid was dismissed until her body was discovered. Had she been on holiday, or had she been closeted with someone from Africa, and had he been driven beyond the limits of endurance?

As yet, this was a question he couldn't answer. And why the hell, he wondered, as his wife lay sleeping peacefully beside him, should anyone want to be bitched and beaten by a tart, and pay good money for the disgrace? Accustomed as he was to deviant human behaviour Cook couldn't find the answer to this question either.

While Cook was lying awake in a semi–detached house, pondering unanswerable questions, Samson was also awake in his flat in a run–down inner-city area. A few hours earlier he had visited Simon Jones who lived on the other side of the river Thames in a third-floor studio flat.

Jones wore heavy-rimmed spectacles which emphasised an abstracted look often to be seen on those who are living half in the real world and half in a private world of their own creation. When the real world had intruded in the massive shape of Samson the customary look of abstraction was ruffled by annoyance at an unscheduled interruption.

'Yes?' he said sharply.

'My name is John Samson. I am a private investigator.' Samson held out a card.

Ignoring the card, the young man said, 'What do you want?'

'A few words with you, if I may.'

'I'm very busy. Highly inconvenient. What is it?'

Samson put the card away. 'Perhaps I could call at a more convenient time. It is important and, I think, will be of particular interest to you.'

In what seemed to be a nervous mannerism Jones licked his lower lip and then rubbed it against the edge of his top teeth. Samson waited for a more verbal reaction. It came in a rush of words. 'Just tell me what it's all about. What's the subject-matter?'

'Briefly, prostitutes. More specifically, the type which specialises in domination. I was advised to come to you by Mrs Vanessa Vincent, an old friend of mine.'

'Oh, well, I suppose you'd better come in but it would have been much better if you'd phoned me first.'

'So sorry,' said Samson stepping nimbly inside.

69

The single room which served as bedroom and sitting room with kitchenette annexe was littered with papers, colour-coded box files, books, newspaper cuttings, cassette tapes, and all the incidental paraphernalia of a dedicated researcher who cared nothing for material disorder so long as his research resulted in an authoritative tome with perfectly ordered cross-references and indices. There were papers spread across the draining board in the kitchenette while a pyramid of dirty dishes was stacked in the sink.

The room reeked of stale tobacco and although it was late on a warm afternoon the windows were closed and a Venetian blind pulled half down. The only concession to decoration was a framed set of cigarette cards showing film stars of the 1930s and a framed publicity photograph of Jane Fonda and Vanessa Redgrave smiling at each other. These hung on each side of a portable television set.

Simon Jones swept some papers off a stool and deposited them on an unmade bed. 'Have a seat, Mr Samson.' Then he went to the window and pulled up the blind revealing a panoramic view over Hampstead Heath and across north-west London. Sunlight exposed a film of dust on the top surface of the television set. From the breast pocket of his shirt Jones extracted a packet of cigarettes, lighted one and sat on the side of the bed.

'Now then, what's this about?'

'I need information about the late Maxine Eastbank. I'll happily pay for it.'

'Oh, Christ!' Jones dragged on the cigarette, blew out smoke and began biting his lip.

'You know of her, I believe.'

'I've been dreading something like this. I don't want to get mixed up in it. I hope you don't think I was a client of hers.'

'I understand you interviewed her for your researches.'

'That's absolutely true. But would the police believe that?'

Samson gazed around the disordered room. 'I think they would, if they saw all this.'

'I hold strong views about the police and their brutal methods of questioning,' said Jones darkly. 'Anyway, I couldn't be of any help to you. I only saw her twice and the last time was eight days before she died. . . . You said it was important. Why is it important?'

'This will sound strange,' said Samson. 'Very strange. But I have a client who isn't sure whether he received treatment at Miss Eastbank's hands, or whether it was some other woman. He has employed me to find out all I can about her. Because Mrs Vincent is an old friend – I helped her once – I went to her first of all. She couldn't really tell me anything except that the lady in question was generally known as Maxine the Man-Tamer, but she did refer me to you.'

Jones flicked the ash from his cigarette. It missed the ashtray and floated to the carpet.

'Maxine was most helpful. At first I thought she wouldn't co-operate but she turned out to be one of the best.' Recollection fired the eyes behind the spectacles. 'She was intelligent. She gave me marvellous material. Epitomised the whole scene. She'll be a key authority in my work.'

'And what's the whole scene about?' asked Samson.

'In a word, power. Adler was right, you know. But there's much more to it than that. Have you read B.F. Skinner's *The Design of Cultures*?'

'For some reason that book has escaped my notice,' said Samson.

'In Skinner's view the slave controls the master as completely as the master controls the slave. It's a very fine psychic balance which is rewarding to both parties. The master – or in Maxine's case the mistress – has power and control over another human being and if that human being is from a superior class, or social status, it will give her a terrific ego-boost. The slave, on the other hand, will choreograph the performance. If he wants pain, it is pain he will get. If he wants verbal abuse, that's what he'll get. If he wants isolation in a darkened room, that's what he'll get. You may ask why anyone should want such humiliation inflicted on him.' Jones looked at Samson searchingly like a tutor regarding a pupil.

Samson knew that if he was to obtain what he wanted he must play along with this fanatical young man. 'Why?' he asked.

'It's the upper and professional classes,' exclaimed Jones in a triumphant voice. 'They have guilt, and well they might, and they purge their guilt by going to people like Maxine. You don't get blue-collar workers going to her.'

Samson resisted the impulse to say, 'They probably couldn't afford her.' Instead, in a wondering voice, he said, 'Perhaps

71

that's why it's never appealed to me. I belong to the working class.'

'Obviously.'

'But surely people like Maxine have other interests? They can't spend all their time enjoying a sort of spurious power over guilty middle- and upper-class men.'

Jones gave a mirthless laugh. 'They do eat and sleep. No, seriously, Maxine told me that recently she'd become very concerned about the welfare of animals. It's a paradox. The woman who gains pleasure – and money, let's face it – from the male of her own species is concerned with the fate of other species. Although she is cruel to her own species, she doesn't want cruelty inflicted on other species by experimentation, culling, or capture for exhibition. Can you see the connection?'

'Connection?'

'The big businessman or the peer goes to her for punishment for his guilt, but what does she do about her own guilts? She campaigns – or used to campaign, I should say – for and on behalf of our dumb friends.' He stubbed out his cigarette and looked proudly at Samson as if at a stroke he had solved not only the riddle of the universe, but every lesser riddle.

'Extraordinary,' said the detective unemotionally. 'Did she belong to any particular group or organisation?'

'I've no idea. She didn't say. Anyway, that's beyond my terms of reference. I only mention it because it happened to come out in conversation with her and you asked about her extra-mural activities.' Jones lighted another cigarette.

'She didn't mention any friends or associates in the same movement?'

'She may have done. In passing. I don't remember. That sort of thing really doesn't interest me much. I think the class struggle is far more important.'

Samson indicated the cassette tapes. 'Is the interview on one of those?'

Jones gave the laugh which was void of any trace of amusement. 'Oh, no. That's all confidential. I'm not going to play that or part with it. Anyway, what is it to this punter of yours if she did mention anyone else, and I can't remember that she did.'

'He might like to help the group,' said Samson.

'Why?'

'He was very impressed by whoever gave him the treatment.'

'Help the group? In what way?'

'A donation perhaps.'

'You surprise me. Most punters are very backward in coming forward. I've had quite a job getting any interviews with them. Could you give me your man's name?'

Samson shook his head sadly. 'I'm afraid not. Like you, I'm bound by confidentiality.'

'Is he a Tory?'

'I don't know.'

'Most of the punters are to the right politically. Did you know that?'

'I didn't.'

'The other side of the fascist coin. Hitler was like it. Fromm refers to an incident in *The Anatomy of Human Destructiveness*. You may have read it.'

Samson shook his head. 'That's another gap in my education, I fear.'

'Apparently Hitler invited Renée Müller, a film star, to the Chancellery one night. After she'd been there for a while he fell at her feet and begged her to kick him. When she obliged he said that being kicked by her was better than he deserved.'

'Remarkable,' said Samson. It was a word he only used when wishing to express polite comment. 'Remarkable' was a perfect vehicle for non-committal opinion, meaningless and yet having the appearance of meaning. 'Remarkable,' he repeated. 'But if we could return for a moment to Miss Eastbank's support of animal welfare, did she mention a friend or animal rights campaigner called Cindy?'

Jones removed the cigarette from his mouth and began biting his lip, deep in thought. After a pause he said, 'The name rings one or two bells but not in connection with Maxine.'

'I think she may have belonged to the same profession.'

Jones was about to say something but stopped. 'Sorry, can't help,' he said.

'Would a donation towards your project refresh your memory?'

'Don't try to bribe me,' replied Jones in an offended voice.

'Bribe? That wasn't my intention. Incidentally, I'm sure the police would be interested in your project, and in your knowledge of Miss Eastbank. And they wouldn't insult you by offering to pay for information.'

'I've told you, I don't want to get mixed up with that. And why should I help the tools of an oppressive capitalist system?' He gave Samson a quick look and lowering his voice added, 'I could tell you something about the police as punters.'

'I daresay you could. And I'm sure the police would like to hear it . . . or get to hear of your views.'

Jones jerked as if he'd been shot and the cigarette fell from his fingers. 'Is that a threat?' He stooped and picked up the cigarette from the carpet.

'Of course not. I've no intention of telling them your opinion of them. But, if I may, I'll leave my card with you, and if your memory of a certain Cindy returns I'd be grateful if you'd get in touch.'

Samson took out his card and placed it on top of the television set.

'I was wrong. The name doesn't ring any bells.'

'It's none of my business,' said Samson, 'but I'm curious. What gave you the idea for studying this subject?'

Jones looked at him warily, stubbed out his cigarette, and stood up.

'If you want to know, it was Rousseau. Jean-Jacques, not *le douanier*. In a sense he was the father of the French and Russian revolutions. His work and life have been a great influence on me. And I've always been intrigued by that passage early on in his *Confessions* where he describes his feelings as a boy for his governess, Mademoiselle Lambercier. I expect you know it.'

'I'm afraid not. It's another example of my deplorable ignorance.'

'Well, after the first chastisement at her hands he found the punishment increased his affection for the inflicter. And later he writes that to fall on his knees before a masterful mistress gave him the most delicate of pleasures.'

'I was under the impression that Rousseau was to the left rather than the right politically. Yet you say most punters are to the right.'

'Rousseau wasn't a punter,' came the indignant reply. 'He was a great man. He influenced Tolstoy, Proust and Goethe, apart from French and Russian radicals.'

Samson smiled, bestowing the benefit of pearly teeth and pink

74

gums on the young man. 'Good day, Mr Jones, and good luck with your polemic.'

'You're not going to the police, are you?'

Samson's smile expanded and he laughed. 'Certainly not.'

Recalling the meeting as he lay awake gazing blankly at a milky wedge of light thrown on the ceiling by a street-lamp, Samson felt increasingly sure that Simon Jones had withheld information which would have helped him. If Phelan had been set up and put under pressure by an extreme animal rights group which had prostitutes among its members it gave a new twist to the cliché about golden-hearted whores.

He could now rule out the possibility that two different women were involved; Maxine Eastbank was certainly the woman who had tried to discipline Phelan like a circus animal. But this knowledge brought him no nearer solving why Phelan should have been dumped close to the dead woman's body and who were the perpetrators of the kidnapping. The other two women still had to be found and possibly one of these was Cindy.

Apart from tracing two women, a wrist-watch had to be recovered, and he was devoid of fresh ideas, leads or hunches. He'd have to plug away at animal welfare organisations and hope to uncover the group, and this could be a long and tedious process. What he needed was a lucky break.

On the other side of the city, Detective Inspector Cook was lying awake and thinking exactly the same thing.

And in a bedroom, roughly halfway between Samson and Cook, Paul Phelan was sleeping beside Cindy.

CHAPTER 9

Unlike most of Samson's clients who, once they had unloaded a problem, were content to await results, Phelan had decided to make some independent enquiries of his own. While the fat detective concentrated on tracing three perverted women, he would try to find the woman who might have played the part of a female Judas, a Judasene. He felt certain that if he roamed London's West End each night he would eventually meet Cindy or someone who knew her.

He started with the bar where they had first met but she wasn't there and the barman didn't remember her. Next he went to a dimly lit basement club in Soho. Almost at once a girl dressed in leather mini-skirt and T-shirt patterned with black and green guitars came and sat at his table. 'Buy me a drink?' she asked.

She had the lost look of an abandoned orphan. 'Sure,' he said.

A topless waitress came across and poured out two glasses of champagne and placed the bottle in an ice-bucket.

Phelan asked the girl how long she'd been working in the club.

'A week.'

'Then you won't know someone called Cindy, or do you?'

'No, I don't.'

Phelan sipped the champagne. 'Fizzy apple juice,' he said and peered at the label on the bottle. 'Never heard of it.'

A girl with a tray filled with plastic dolls approached the table. Phelan waved her away.

'I'd like one of them,' said his companion.

Phelan looked at her. 'I'm not surprised. Does your family know you're here?'

'Christ, no.'

He looked around. At another table three men were being

entertained by girls; there seemed to be more fondling, slapping and laughter than talk.

The girl with the tray of dolls approached again from a different direction and Phelan didn't see her until she was at the table.

'I'd love one of them, please,' said his companion and there was more desperation than desire in her voice.

Phelan turned to the girl selling dolls. 'Do you know someone called Cindy?' he asked.

'Can't say I do.'

'You can take that stuff away,' he said. 'I don't want any of it.' He looked back at the sad girl seated beside him. 'Take my tip, go home,' he said. 'No offence, but I have to be moving on. You can finish the apple juice. I'll get the bill.'

He signalled to the bar and moments later the topless waitress brought a slip of paper on a tarnished nickel-silver salver. The bill was for seventy pounds.

'I'm not paying seventy,' said Phelan and he calmly tore up the slip of paper. He tossed a five-pound note on the table. 'That's more than what it was worth. Good night, sweetheart.'

His way to the exit was barred by two burly men whose suits fitted too tightly across the chest. One of them said, 'Leaving without paying. That would be a great mistake.'

If a fight was inevitable it was always best to get in the first blow. Phelan hit the man hard in the stomach and as he jack-knifed caught him under the chin with his other fist. Using the momentum of the blow to side-step he stamped hard on the foot of the other man and brought his free knee up hard into the man's groin. It was as perfectly executed as a ballet sequence and as a *coup de grâce* he gave the first man a karate chop. Then he pushed through a swing door and walked up a flight of stairs to the street.

A punk with a coxcomb of crimson hair asked him for a light. Phelan said, 'I don't have one. Do you, by any chance, know a woman called Cindy?'

The punk grinned. 'I'm a stranger here meself, mate. But if you want a bit of black try the Basalt in Greek Street.'

Phelan moved on through a loitering gaggle of tourists who seemed spellbound by garish illuminations and lights that flashed 'Striptease'.

He crossed to the other side of the road and made his way

along a crowded sidewalk to a sign which in blue neon spelled out 'The Twenty-Seven Club'.

The receptionist at this club at first refused admission as he wasn't a member but a ten-pound note overcame this statutory requirement. It was a drinking club with alcoves, two chandeliers, and plaster statues of nude women in the classical style of Praxiteles. Fleshy men and hard-eyed women wearing too much make-up seemed to constitute the club's clientele. A hubbub of chatter wrestled for supremacy with speakers relaying taped music.

Phelan made his way to the bar and ordered a whisky on the rocks. He caught the eye of a lone woman, dark-eyed, dark-haired with pointed features. Phelan smiled at her. She smiled back. Soon they were talking. He asked his standard question.

The woman laughed. 'Why? You lost her?'

'Sort of.'

'Yeah, I know Cindy. Sinful Cindy.' She laughed again. 'Cindy Chopolski.'

'I don't know her other name.'

'You don't? Well, isn't that something.'

'Where can I find her?'

'Where? You've come to the right place.'

'What do you mean?'

'What do I mean,' the woman laughed, and it was a laugh which was beginning to grate on Phelan. 'I mean what I say. You've come to the right place. Use your eyes. She's sitting over there with Poncho, but I don't recommend you to intrude, not unless you want to be chivved.'

Phelan looked in the direction she indicated and saw a fey-like woman with red hair in animated conversation with a bull of a man.

'That's not the Cindy I'm looking for,' he said.

'She's not? Great.' The woman reached out a hand which had blood-red fingernails and she delicately stroked his thigh. 'Maybe I stand a chance.'

'No,' he said. 'You don't.'

He knocked back his drink. 'Good night, sweetheart.'

After the seventh bar he decided to return to his hotel.

The next evening was a repeat performance and again he drew a blank. On the following evening he was tempted by a girl who

78

reminded him of Isabella. She had the same slightly slanted eyes and the same uninhibited, wide, white smile. But her hair was in West Indian dreadlocks and she spoke with a cockney accent and this dispelled the illusion that with her he might be back in central Africa, and he realised that his nostalgia wouldn't be appeased by a night entwined in her arms and legs. But he spent time and money on her and when they parted it was as friends. He had slipped a note into her hand and said, 'That's for your taxi fare,' and she had replied, 'You're a gentleman. I envy Cindy, whoever she is.'

Although the media were losing interest in the murder of Maxine Eastbank, Phelan was still being harassed by anonymous phone calls and poison-pen letters but because he didn't like to be driven out by such pressures he delayed switching hotels. A less obstinate man, stubbornly determined not to waver in his purpose, would either have gone into hiding or left the country.

While his evenings were spent searching for Cindy in various bars, during the day he would either hire a car and drive out of town or go for long walks along the Thames embankment. He visited Whipsnade zoo on the Dunstable Downs as well as the safari park near Windsor, and on foot he went to Regent's Park zoo and the Natural History Museum at Kensington. But none of these activities brought much satisfaction; he was simply passing time until the evening search.

He grew increasingly bored with London and almost for the first time in his life he wished there was a place he could call 'home'. All his adult life had been nomadic but without the security of a fixed star to travel by or move towards. He wondered what it would be like to settle somewhere permanently and the thought was tinged with wistfulness.

Whenever he called Samson the news was always the same: nothing to report. And then Samson called him and they met in the Eros bar of the Piccadilly Hotel. By then he'd decided to make a temporary home in Karen's house where, he hoped, he'd be free from the attentions of protesters. It was shortly after leaving Samson, when he was at a pedestrian crossing near the Royal Academy, waiting for lights to change, that a delighted female voice exclaimed, 'Paul!'

He turned and saw Cindy. The pleasure in her voice shone in her eyes.

79

The traffic lights changed but they both stood still, a small breakwater in the surging sea of humanity which flooded across the street.

Her pleasure faded under his coldly impassive gaze. 'What's the matter,' she asked. 'You remember me?'

'I remember you.'

'I know it was only a night but . . .'

'I've been wanting to see you again,' he said.

She brightened momentarily. 'You have?'

'Some questions need answers.'

'What? . . . Here? . . .'

He took her arm and piloted her through traffic which was beginning to edge forward. A man in a Mercedes blasted the car-horn and they were almost hit by a bus travelling in the reverse direction in a bus lane.

'That was hairy,' she said as they reached the safety of the opposite sidewalk.

'I thought you liked living dangerously.'

'Me? Not particularly.'

'Then you should change the company you keep.'

They were facing each other and looked like a couple on the brink of a quarrel.

'What on earth do you mean by that?' she asked.

'I'll tell you, but not here. We're near the park. Coming?'

She hesitated. 'All right then, but I've got an appointment with a dentist at three.'

'This shouldn't take long.'

They went without speaking past the Ritz and entered Green Park where, enjoying the Indian summer, people were scattered over the grass like splashes of colour on a slack green canvas. Some reclined in hired deck-chairs while others squatted and ate lunchtime snacks. A few, like Phelan and Cindy, were on the footpath.

He slowed his pace and said, 'Where were you when I was being attacked?'

'Attacked?'

'Don't play dumb. You must have seen.'

'I don't know what you're talking about. Is it the night after the television when you suddenly ran off?'

'It is,' he replied drily.

'I'll tell you what happened. You charged off, just like that.

80

No explanation. I started to run after you but I was tripped. I went flying.'

'You tripped?' he asked sceptically.

'I *was* tripped.' She stopped. 'You don't believe me.' Pointing at her left shin she said, 'Look!'

He saw the fading marks of a graze.

'It ruined a pair of tights and shook me up. If that's of the slightest interest to you.' The shine in her eyes had become a glare. 'Now, what's your excuse?'

'Excuse? I don't have to make excuses.'

'Oh, yes, you do. If you've dragged me here to answer some damn questions, you've got an excuse to make first. Why did you bolt?'

Phelan was nonplussed. If all men were natural enemies it was also true that all women were natural actresses. Like many European men of his generation who had lived many years in central Africa he believed women fell into three categories. They might be sexual challenges, or they were ciphers who wore a tribal tag like Bantu or Bahutu, or they were female counterparts of fellow Europeans who had to be treated as gentle extensions of their male protectors. But to whatever category they belonged they could never be trusted; they were all potential Oscar-winning actresses.

'I didn't bolt,' he said. 'My pocket was picked. I got my wallet back but someone gave me a jab and I was carted away in a car. It was all pre-planned.'

'And you think I had something to do with that?' Her voice quivered with suppressed anger.

'Didn't you?'

She wasn't tall but she increased in stature as, with head held back, she looked him up and down disdainfully. 'I thought you were someone special but you're nothing more than a stupid self-opinionated man. A bull in a china shop has more finesse than you. Good day, Mr Phelan.'

She swung smartly on her heels and marched away. He caught up with her and grabbed her arm. 'Just a minute.'

She shook herself free. 'If you don't leave me alone,' she hissed, 'I shall scream "Rape!"'

'Listen. When I got free after two days in a hell-hole I went to your flat. You'd never been heard of. How do you explain that?'

'I don't have to explain anything to you. And it's nonsense to

81

say I'd never been heard of. I've had that flat for more than three years and everyone on the floor knows me.'

A doubt crossed his mind. 'What's its address?'

'What address did you try?'

'Number forty-two Greenhill Mansions.'

'I'm not surprised they'd never heard of me. I live in Greenacre Court. Goodbye.'

'Cindy!' He hurried after her.

'Don't pester me.'

It was never easy to say 'Sorry' but he did. 'I'm sorry. I apologise. I made a mistake.'

'You certainly did.' She slowed down. 'I feel pity for you. It must be terrible to go through life thinking the worst of everybody, never the best.'

She had slowed to a halt. A small boy, running, and without looking where he was going, collided with her. She caught and held him to her as if he were a food parcel thrown to a refugee. A woman called, 'You come here, you little devil.'

The boy smiled at Cindy and, dragging his feet, returned to his mother.

'I have another question,' said Phelan.

'What?'

'That night we met.'

'What about it?'

'Why were you there?'

'It's none of your business, but I'll tell you. I'd been let down. It doesn't often happen, I assure you. I was waiting for someone who didn't turn up.'

'I'm glad he didn't.'

'It wasn't a "he"; it was a "she".'

'I thought . . .'

'You thought I was a prostitute.'

'You took my money.'

'And why not? You raised the subject. You asked what I wanted for my "present". If that isn't the same as asking "How much?" I don't know what is. I could either have told you not to insult me or stung you for what I thought I could get. I decided to sting you. But I didn't charge you for staying on, if you remember.'

He was silent.

82

'Women can go alone into bars these days,' she said, 'and meet other women there.'

'Yes.'

They stood looking at each other, no longer a couple on the verge of a quarrel, but a couple about to make it up.

'Let me make amends for my mistake,' said Phelan. 'Come and have a drink or something to eat.'

'I'm not hungry or thirsty, thanks. And I've got a dental appointment.'

'Can I see you again?'

She gave him a long, appraising look. 'OK,' she said at length, 'so I do sleep around a bit. Is that what you want? My beautiful body?'

'I like your company. Your conversation.'

'You could have fooled me.'

'I've said I'm sorry.'

'All right, we'll meet again. Where and when?'

At that time he had no intention of bringing her back to Karen's house. He said, 'I'll meet you in the foyer of the Piccadilly Hotel at seven tonight.'

'I'll be there.'

He watched her as she walked away with the confident step of a woman sure of her own identity and her right to be totally independent.

The evening went well and when eventually she laughed and said, 'Your place or mine?' he surprised her by saying, 'Mine.' After a pause he added, 'It's not my home – I don't have one – but it's on loan from a friend and better than offering you a hotel room. Of course, if you'd prefer to go to your place...'

'No, we'll go to yours.'

It didn't seem quite moral to take her back to the house of his former wife, but morality was just an uncomfortable human concept; it wasn't a survival necessity.

Later, and before they went to sleep, he told her about his experiences in the cage. She listened in silence and when he had finished said, 'If I can help you find them, I will.'

'I don't see how you can.'

'Leave it to me. I have contacts.'

CHAPTER 10

Information on the domination scene was carefully collated by the police in the hope that a clue would emerge pointing to the possible killer of Maxine Eastbank. A number of dominatrices were interviewed and some, under threat of prosecution for offences not directly related to their profession, were willing to provide names of men who had visited them. They referred to diaries and notebooks and divulged the names and addresses of all their visitors. In return the threat of prosecution was waived.

An astute young constable running the names through a computer noticed the recurrence of a name belonging to someone who was a caller as distinct from a client. The name was Simon Jones and undercover enquiries revealed that he was collecting data on women who practised domination techniques. The constable referred his finding to a senior officer who telephoned Cook.

'We've come across a young fellow – a perennial student you might call him – who reckons he's collecting facts on every fladge merchant in town. He might know something about the Man-Tamer, her m.o., if you like, something new that you wouldn't get from a punter.'

Cook sensed that a lucky break might be peeping around the corner. 'Thanks. Let's have his name and address, and anything else you've got on him.'

Within an hour he was on his way to Simon Jones's flat accompanied by Detective Sergeant Wilkins.

They were used to cool receptions but hadn't expected to be greeted by white-faced horror when Cook announced their names and said they were conducting an investigation into a murder. It looked as if the researcher was about to faint. In a strained voice he said, 'I can account fully for all my movements and if you're going to question me I want a lawyer present.'

'I doubt if that will be necessary, Mr Jones,' said Cook in his friendly watch–carefully–children party voice. 'Surely you won't want to be paying unnecessary legal fees but if you want a solicitor after you've heard what we've got to say you can call him.' He paused before continuing in a less friendly voice, 'But if you do, I have to advise you that the interview will have to take place in the nearest police station.' After allowing this ultimatum to sink in he said, 'May we come in?'

Jones wiped his brow with the back of his hand and began chewing his lip. The two detectives waited for his reply. At last it came. 'Oh, all right. Come in. But it's highly inconvenient. I'm very busy.'

'We shan't detain you long,' said Cook and he walked into the flat. 'My word, you are a busy man. What exactly is your business, Mr Jones?'

'You must know. That's why you're here, isn't it?'

'But I'd like to hear your version.'

Jones sat down on the only available space, a corner of an unmade bed. He didn't clear any litter to provide his visitors with a seat.

'I'm on a research project, a sociological treatise in the form of a thesis, in which the corrupting influence of capitalism is exposed in its most basic and obscene form. I am studying the dynamics of prostitution of a special kind, the kind that appeals to guilt-laden capitalists who are exploited by women who could be called proto-capitalists themselves. Does that answer your question?'

Cook nodded. 'It goes some way. One of your so-called proto-capitalists was a woman called Maxine Eastbank.'

Colour which had been returning to Jones's face ebbed away. 'I knew it. That man Samson tipped you off, didn't he? And the bastard said he wouldn't.'

Cook remained stolidly still and his face gave nothing away but Wilkins shifted his stance and gave his senior a quick look.

'The only Samson I know of,' said Cook, 'was deceived by a lady called Delilah who on one occasion took some new ropes and bound him. Don't tell me you've been interviewing two ghosts on the question of Old Testament bondage.'

Jones recovered enough nerve to retort, 'Oh, very droll. You know damn well who he is.'

'Maybe I do, but I'd like you to tell me, if you'd be so kind.'

Jones sprang up and went to the television set. He picked up Samson's card from its top and thrust it at Cook. 'That's your Samson.'

Cook looked at the card and put it in his pocket. 'Why did this Samson call on you?'

'You bloody well know. You're trying to frame me for something.' Jones's voice rose in angry excitement. 'He was trying to draw me out about Maxine Eastbank. He gave me some guff about having a client, some guy who was sympathetic to her. Ridiculous. I think he was an agent for some punter, although he denied it, and was hoping to shift the blame on to me. He hoped I'd implicate myself in some way so as to get his client off the hook, but I didn't, and so now you've come to try and pressurise me.' Words poured out in a rush of nervous defiance. 'You can save your time. I've got a watertight alibi. I was in Sheffield with my auntie May on the night. I was nowhere near London. But if you try to intimidate my aunt and she collapses – she has a heart condition – I shall sue you to the limit. I shall get my MP on the case and I shall make sure the press is given another example of police brutality and harassment.'

Jones was breathless with the effort of accusation. He sat, panting, like someone who had just run against a gale force wind and driving rain to catch a train.

'I don't think it will be necessary,' said Cook with the measured step of someone who would sooner wait for the next train than hurry, 'to interview auntie May so we won't put the ambulance service on stand-by. But I should like to ask you about Miss Eastbank. It won't take long. Speaking of which, do you have the correct time? I seem to have left my watch at home.'

Jones glanced down. 'It's ten to eleven.'

'Nice watch that. Had it some time, have you?'

'This? It's a cheapie. I bought it from a friend who got it in Hong Kong.' Jones extended his arm. 'Have a good look. It should interest you. It's a forgery.'

Cook bent down and looked. 'Cartier.'

'Exactly. A replica of a watch that should sell for more than a thousand but it costs just twenty pounds in Hong Kong. But the originators can't be prosecuted because they've left off the period, or fullstop, after the word "Cartier" on the dial and that

86

makes it a different product.' He looked up at Cook. 'Hong Kong is the most intensive capitalist-orientated society in the world, and like all capitalist societies it thrives on fraud.'

'Thanks for the political lesson,' said Cook drily. 'Now, can we get down to basics? I'd be grateful if you'd tell me all you know about Maxine Eastbank. I may be a brutal instrument of a foul capitalist society but I imagine that you, like me, would want her killer found. We do have that in common, if nothing else.' In an undertone he added, 'Thank God.'

'I heard that!'

'Did you now? And what are you going to do about it? Treat me to a monologue on God not existing but being invented by capitalists to keep the poor in their place?'

'You can be as sarcastic as you like. I'm not going to be drawn. I'm not going to give you an excuse to beat me up.'

'Please, Mr Jones. Keep to the point. Do you want a killer found?'

'Of course I do.'

'Then tell me everything you can.'

After a moment's thought Jones reached for a file lying near the bed pillow.

'It's all in here. She was a human being, you know. And she wasn't simply interested in her job. She contributed anonymously to a donkey sanctuary and she was concerned for the welfare of dumb animals.'

Cook gave a thin smile. 'Dumb animals. Yes, her punters were pretty dumb. They are the dumb animals I'm interested in. Who did she know, professionally and otherwise?'

'She didn't tell me and I didn't ask. If you want names, you can go elsewhere. She didn't name names.'

'How very honourable of her. Would you care to lend me your file? I'll give you a receipt.'

'No way,' snapped Jones, his confidence restored. 'You'll have to get a court order first.'

'Maybe I shall do just that.' Cook turned to Wilkins. 'I don't think we need delay Mr Jones any further. Have you any questions?'

'No, sir.'

'Then we'll bid you good day, Mr Jones.'

Once outside the flat Cook said, 'We must find out everything we can about this Samson and then we'll pay him a visit. I'll bet he's been hired by an interested party. And what I'd like to know is why the party in question is sufficiently interested to hire a private eye.'

From his office Cook telephoned New Scotland Yard and spoke to a colleague. He asked what was known about John Samson and was told that Samson had been helpful in the past, was a contributor to the Police Benevolent Fund, and should not be leaned on too heavily.

'I lean gently like the tower of Pisa,' said Cook.

'Did you say you were leaning like a pisser?' came the instant reply.

'That's a bad joke,' said Cook, and he rang off.

Although he liked making puns he didn't care to have them made at his expense. To Wilkins he said, 'Right. We'll pay Mr Samson a call.'

CHAPTER 11

When, some years before, Samson had inherited a small private enquiry agency on the death of an uncle he found the business was little more than a run-down debt-collecting agency. He worked hard to expand into wider fields and cut down on debt-collecting. Although he didn't object to exerting pressure on bad payers who had means, he much disliked moving against people living on the poverty line who had over-extended themselves by entering hire-purchase agreements which they couldn't possibly afford to maintain.

With the reduction of the debt-collecting side of his business he was able to take on more cases involving missing persons and matrimonial enquiries. But when the divorce laws were amended, and hard evidence of adultery was seldom required, he took on work as a security adviser and, more recently, investigations relating to directors of large corporations when a company take-over was in the wind.

In the last month he had advised on security for a company which had two large warehouses in the district and sold cheap furniture. The company, satisfied with his advice, was now asking if he'd undertake some debt-collecting business for them. If so, further lucrative commissions could come his way. He was weighing the advantages and disadvantages of this inducement when Shandy walked into his room and, after closing the door behind her, came up to his desk. In a voice which even the keenest ear pressed to a door wouldn't hear she said, 'I've got two cops from CID out there. They want to see you.'

'What about?'

'They won't say. It's confidential.'

Samson thought for a moment. 'I don't like it. The CID. Are they on to Phelan, I wonder? Do they know I'm acting for him?'

It was a rhetorical question. Shandy waited for him to continue.

'Because if they are, I wouldn't put it past them to put a tap on our phones. I'll see them, but you slip upstairs and put a call through to Phelan and tell him not to contact me. I'll contact him.'

Samson had an arrangement with an elderly woman who lived above his office and eked out a meagre living by embroidering linen. When he suspected his phone might be tapped he would make calls from her room. For this service he paid her telephone rental and, more often than not, her entire bill.

'Will do,' said Shandy. 'Shall I show them in?'

Samson stood up and straightened his tie. 'Yes. And ask if they'd like coffee.' The shadow of a smile came to his lips. 'I shall offer them something stronger but they'll have to refuse and they'll hate that. I've never yet met a CID man who isn't a heavy drinker.'

Before Shandy left the room Samson checked that his tape recorder was operating. It was linked from a drawer to an hour-glass which stood on his desk and in its base contained a microphone which could pick up sound in any part of the room.

When Shandy had introduced the visitors as Detective Inspector Cook and Detective Sergeant Wilkins she left to put in a call to Phelan from upstairs.

Samson indicated chairs of different shapes and sizes which lined the wall in front of a row of stilled clocks. 'Please sit down and let me get you a drink.'

'No, thanks. We've already declined your secretary's offer of coffee.'

'I've got something better than coffee,' said Samson. 'A good selection of whiskies or, if you prefer, gin or vodka.'

'Thank you, no,' replied Cook firmly. 'I would have thought,' he went on as if musing aloud, 'that you would know we never touch the hard stuff on duty.'

Samson affected surprise. 'Oh, this is duty, is it? I thought you might have come to sell me tickets for the annual prize draw in aid of police dependants. I always take a couple of booklets but never win.'

'I'm afraid we've come on more serious business.'

Looking disappointed, Samson sat down in his swivel chair. 'More serious than police dependants. And nothing to do with the Police Benevolent Fund either, I assume. I contribute to that too.'

'You are correct.'

'It must be serious.'

'We regard murder as serious.'

Samson feigned surprise once more. 'Murder? Whose murder?'

'Come now, Mr Samson,' said Cook equably. 'Don't beat about the bush. You must know very well whose murder.'

Samson appeared to think deeply. 'I have a vague idea,' he said at length, 'and I would like to co-operate as I always do. But if you want my co-operation there must be no bush-beating on your part either.'

As he spoke he tipped the hour-glass so that the sand would pass through a glass channel from one transparent chamber to the other. In doing so he was able to adjust the base in what seemed a natural movement so that the microphone was turned in Cook's direction. The detective, apparently to avoid a shaft of sunlight coming through the window, had moved his chair to a corner of the room before sitting down. Wilkins stayed put; he opened a briefcase which rested on his lap and took out a notebook.

'Taxi drivers have their meters,' Samson went on. 'This is my meter. It takes exactly half an hour for the sand to trickle through, and half an hour is the most I can afford you.'

'I hope we shan't keep you that long,' said Cook, 'but I'm interested in your collection here.' He glanced round at the clocks. 'I expect you're a bit of an expert on these.'

'A bit of an expert.'

'You know quite a bit about watches too, I expect.'

'I know a little, but they don't interest me as much.'

'You wear one yourself?'

Samson pulled back his coat sleeve to reveal three watches. 'You'll probably recognise the top one,' he said. 'Not really a watch at all but a silent motorised camera. I hardly ever use it, but I rather like gadgetry.'

Cook glanced at his own watch. 'Mine's a digital but I've always fancied having a quality one.' He paused and looked unblinkingly at Samson. 'Would you call a Rolex oyster a quality watch?'

By contrast, Samson's eyes closed slightly as if he were brooding on the question. 'I wouldn't spend the money if I were you, if it's simply time-keeping you want, but if you want a status symbol I suppose it has merits.'

Although on one level he was giving a considered opinion on a watch, on a different level he was wondering why the police were letting him know they possessed facts which could affect his client. It was too much of a coincidence that Phelan's watch was a Rolex oyster. Did they know Phelan's identity and were trying to discover his whereabouts, or were they probing for information on someone who had lost a watch and, if so, why? The watch must be linked, probably as a piece of evidence, to the murder of Maxine Eastbank. How did they know that he, Samson, might be able to help in their investigations?

These thoughts raced through his mind as he sat back in a relaxed, almost indolent, way in his chair.

'Yes, the Rolex oyster has its merits. As for myself, I've never been particularly bothered about status symbols. I've known cases where the symbol gradually possesses the owner rather than the owner possessing the symbol. I knew a man who bankrupted himself and ruined his family life because he was obsessed with owning a Rolls-Royce.' Samson opened his half-closed eyes and met Cook's unwavering gaze. 'But we're straying from the point, I guess.'

'Maybe. But sometimes I think that we in the police force are rather like some other trades, playwrights for instance, where everything seen or heard is grist to the mill. No information is totally useless. One day it could have a bearing on your job or your art. But you're right, we mustn't stray too far from the point.'

'Which is?'

'The murder of Maxine Eastbank.'

'Ah, yes. I've read about that.'

'And enquired about it.'

Cook's remark was a statement, not a question. So, thought Samson, they must have interviewed Jones. How the devil had they got on to him?

'I have made one or two enquiries of an academic nature.' Samson leaned forward over his desk as if to impart a confidence. 'I have a client, a lady of nervous disposition, who was once in the same line of business as Miss Eastbank and who has taken Miss Eastbank's death to heart. She came to me in the hope that I might be able to discover a motive for her murder. I told her this was a criminal matter for the police, and I wouldn't be able to turn up anything which the police wouldn't have turned up before me. But she was insistent. She felt she might be on some maniac's list and might be the next victim.' Samson sighed. 'It's terrible to feel threatened.'

'Would you tell us the name of your client, Mr Samson?'

Samson sat back. 'Certainly not.'

'If we felt there was a serious threat to her life, and there might be, we could arrange for police protection.'

'No.'

'It could be helpful to you personally,' said Cook without a trace of menace in his voice, 'if you felt it your duty to tell us the name of this client, for her own protection. Any action we took would be most discreet.'

'The answer is still no.'

'Then I must infer that your notions of confidentiality are either extremely rigid or that you do indeed have a client with an interest in the case but who is not a lady of nervous disposition. Do I make myself clear?'

'Quite clear.'

Cook crossed one leg over the other. It looked as if he intended to stay until the top chamber of the hour-glass was empty.

'I wonder if you could explain something to me, Mr Samson.'

'I'll try.'

'As you may have guessed we have been having a little chat with a Mr Jones who, as you will know, is something of an authority on women of Maxine Eastbank's sort. He was convinced you represented a male client. At least, that's what you told him. He referred to your client as a punter who was, as he put it, sympathetic to the deceased.'

Cook looked enquiringly at Samson.

'He must have been mistaken.'

'Or perhaps, by some extraordinary coincidence, you have not one, but two clients, who have instructed you with regard to this case. One, a nervous lady, and two, a sympathetic gentleman.'

'Coincidences abound in life,' said Samson. He looked at ease but he realised that in Cook he had a tough opponent and it would take all his wits to outsmart the CID man.

'As someone who operates in the same field as mine you will be well aware of the penalties for wasting police time, Mr Samson.'

'Well aware. But, as I never tire of pointing out, we do not waste Time. Time wastes all of us, even members of our esteemed police force.'

'You will also be aware of the penalties which attach to an accessory after the fact,' Cook continued. 'They invariably result in a custodial sentence in cases of this sort.'

'And quite right too,' Samson said emphatically. 'People who assist murderers or cover up for them, and mislead the police, deserve to go to prison.'

'I'm glad you realise the score. And because you do, I'll give you another opportunity. What is the name of your client, because I know you do have a client.'

'And may have more than one. But as for names, the answer is as before, no.'

'Let's keep it simple. Let's assume you have only one client. A male. Let's also assume that, like most men, he normally wears a watch.'

'A watch? Well, there's another coincidence for you. We were talking about watches only a few minutes ago.'

'We were.'

'Would I be right in thinking a Rolex oyster has something to do with the case?'

Cook uncrossed his legs. Then he straightened his trouser creases. He was uncertain whether to say anything which might be helpful to Samson in protecting his unknown client from police enquiries. If you had a lucky break you had to take care not to dissipate its chances of success by being too forthcoming. On the other hand, too much reticence could be the end of the break. When luck came your way, you had to back it. He turned to his associate. 'Show him,' he said.

Wilkins stood up and produced a watch. He placed it on Samson's desk.

'We are looking for the owner of that,' said Cook. 'Can you assist us, and please think very, very carefully before replying. I don't need to remind you of the penalties for giving false information.'

Samson picked up the watch and examined it. 'It seems to be in good working order but if you want an expert opinion you'd better take it to a watchmaker.'

'You don't know of anyone who may have lost or mislaid such a watch?'

Samson realised at once that the watch must be a piece of

94

evidence and, as such, had been found near Maxine Eastbank's body. He put the deduction into words. 'Was this found near Miss Eastbank's body?'

'It was, and we should like to know how it got there.'

Samson held up the watch by the end of its strap.

'Was it like this? Unfastened? Or was it fastened?'

'Unfastened.'

'The strap is strong and the buckle is big and strong. It couldn't have fallen off by accident. It must have been placed beside the body.'

Wilkins moved forward and took back the watch.

'Perhaps,' said Cook. 'Perhaps not.'

'Placed there by someone who wanted to incriminate its owner,' Samson went on.

Cook laughed. It was a sound not often heard by his colleagues and resembled water gurgling down a plug-hole.

'I can't buy that,' he said. 'If someone wanted to plant incriminating evidence they would use something better than an unidentifiable watch.'

'All the same it's not much use as evidence that its owner, even if traced, was connected with Miss Eastbank's murder.'

'That would be for a jury to decide.'

Samson nodded vigorously. 'I agree. And our jury system is the best in the world. Never a wrongful conviction on planted evidence. Well, hardly ever.'

'I wish you would cooperate with us, Mr Samson. Your client would have every opportunity to clear himself of suspicion.'

'I'm sorry I can't help you.'

Cook stood up. 'The sands of time are running out. We'll be on our way. But if you have any second thoughts I'd be glad if you'd get in touch with us. Otherwise . . .' He left the sentence unfinished.

Samson knew the implication. Cook would do everything in his power to find out who he represented.

He reached out and pressed a button. 'Shandy, would you show these gentlemen out.'

Wilkins put away the notebook which he had hardly used and closed his briefcase.

Cook said, 'Good day. I think we shall meet again.'

Samson peeled back his upper lip in the semblance of a smile. 'I hope so,' he said. 'It's a pleasure to meet you. I always like to

95

help the police whenever I can and I'm sorry professional etiquette prevented me from disclosing the names of any clients.'

When the outer door had been closed by Shandy, Samson hurried across her room to the fridge which stood in one corner beside a small annexe which contained a sink, an immersion heater and an electric ring.

'What are you looking for?' she asked.

'I'm getting some ice. I feel like a large gin and tonic with ice. We haven't got a lemon, have we?'

She shook her head. 'If you're going to switch from your usual I suppose I'd better get one. . . . How did it go?'

'Not very well.' Samson unscrewed the cap from a bottle of tonic water. 'They've got Phelan's watch which was found close to Maxine Eastbank's body. And thanks to that student of capitalist evils they know I represent someone connected with her and they want his name. Did you manage to get through to him?'

'No joy. I let it ring about twenty times. He must be out.'

Samson lifted his glass. 'Would you like one?'

'No, thanks. I'm meeting my husband for lunch today. I'll have one with him. Would you like me to go to Phelan's place? I could slip a note through the letter-box.'

'I'll go myself. He might be back. If not, I'll leave a note. When's your lunch?'

'Now,' she said.

'I'll wait till you get back. Can't leave the office unmanned.'

'If I was a libber I'd say "or unwimmined".'

Samson rubbed his chin reflectively. 'That reminds me. What was her name? Nan Bellman? You saw the show. They didn't hit it off.'

'Right. They didn't. Macho male meets ultra feminist. No Tarzan and Jane idyll.'

'I wouldn't expect a TV presenter, a household name, to be mixed up with this,' said Samson, 'but one can never tell. While I'm out, see what you can find out about her.'

'OK. Can I go now?'

'Have a good lunch.'

Samson returned to his room. Unusually, he wasn't hungry but he had plenty of food for thought. Cook was the sort of police detective who combined the cunning of a fox with the tenacity of a fox terrier. Such men were difficult to shake off once they had scented a quarry. Cook had the circumstantial evidence of Phelan's watch; he had only to find out that a few hours prior to Maxine Eastbank's death she had been humiliating Phelan, and he would possess a motive for murder, a revenge killing by Phelan.

Although he thought it unlikely, Samson couldn't rid himself of the thought that Phelan might have been responsible, might have killed while under the influence of a drug, and then suffered some sort of selective amnesia. Such cases were rare, but they had occurred. The best way to shift the spotlight from Phelan would be to discover someone with an equally strong motive for committing the crime. The most obvious candidate would be one of Maxine Eastbank's clients, but presumably Cook had already exhausted this line of enquiry. Who else would have a motive?

It was a warm day. Samson loosened his collar and went to the fridge for more ice for another gin and tonic. His appetite was activated when he noticed a plate of ham, covered in clingfilm, at the bottom of the fridge. This would provide a snack until he felt the need for a more substantial meal.

Back again at his desk, the plate of ham and slices of bread and butter beside him, he returned to the matter which had occupied his thoughts before the unwelcome appearance of the two police detectives. It didn't take long to decide to turn down the commission for debt-collecting. His foot-in-the-door days were now limited to occasional process-serving and enquiries on behalf of a client. He had finished with hounding improvident live-now-pay-later men and women.

The ham had been finished, and the fridge almost emptied of other edibles by the time Shandy returned.

'Good lunch?' he enquired.

'Lovely.'

'I'll go now.'

'I hope you'll find him in.'

'So do I. Trouble is heading his way. If he's got any sense he'll drop the idea of getting his own back on some silly animal rights group. He'll get out of the country as fast as he can.'

'But will he?'

'I doubt it,' said Samson, 'but we'll see.'

CHAPTER 12

Back at headquarters, Cook considered his next move. He was convinced Samson was protecting someone who had been closely connected with Maxine Eastbank. He turned to Wilkins who was studying the transcript of the interview with Samson. His briefcase, which had rested on his lap during the interview, was fitted with tape recorder and microphone; Cook's move to a corner of the room, apparently to avoid a shaft of sunlight, had been to make himself equidistant between Wilkins and Samson so that volume control could be balanced.

'Cocky sod,' said Cook.

Wilkins, startled, looked up. 'Pardon?'

'Not you, Brian, I was thinking of that slob. Fatty Arbuckle. He tried to get under my skin. I liked the way he tried to teach me my job.' Cook tried to mimic Samson's voice. 'It couldn't have fallen off by accident. It must have been placed near the body.'

'Beside the body.'

'What?'

'He said, "beside the body". Not "near the body".'

'For Christ's sake, don't you start. One lot of provocation today is enough.'

'Sorry.'

'He's covering for someone. No doubt of it. We must find out who. How do we do that, Brian?'

'Tap his phone.'

Cook pulled a reproving face. 'Tut, tut, Sergeant. You know the Home Secretary is having a purge on that sort of thing. The rights of the individual, civil liberty, and all that. But Home Secretaries don't have to do our job, do they? So, yes, we'll tap his phone. And, Brian, I'd like a tail put on him. He's a smart, fat slob and might sus out his line will be tapped and go and see his client in person.'

'Right.'

'So when you've finished – have you much more to do?'

'Not much.'

'When you've finished, see to it, Brian, if you would.'

'Right.'

Cook stood up. 'I've got to go out for a while. Be back in an hour or so.'

Cook deliberately hadn't said where he was going. It wasn't good for discipline for anyone of junior rank to know he needed to buy a prop for a conjuring trick he was planning to perform for the first time at a children's party that evening. If Wilkins, or anyone else, knew about it they'd think he was skiving and feel entitled to do the same. But Cook didn't regard his hobby as skiving; to him it was essential relaxation.

Some men found a necessary release from tension in sex, others in driving fast cars, others in listening to the works of Vivaldi or Verdi. He found it in entertaining little children, in seeing their reactions when he flicked a silk handkerchief and a budgerigar flew out. But kids these days were becoming increasingly difficult to amaze or amuse. A rot had set in with television where high-class professionals, aided by props costing thousands, had baffled studio audiences.

It was while he was paying for a stick with a magnetic tip that he noticed a display of masks in a showcase. Immediately he was dragged back to his job; the temporary escape from routine, his brief period of relaxation, was over. One of the masks was identical to the mask which had covered Maxine Eastbank's eyes.

'Do you get much call for those?' he asked the shopkeeper.

'Not a lot. Not a lot.'

The shopkeeper laughed at the neatness of his own wit in quoting the well-known catchphrase of a popular TV magician. When he saw Cook was unamused he continued, 'There's some demand in winter months for fancy dress balls. And I have one or two customers who need them for a different profession, if you follow me.'

'Ladies of easy virtue?'

'You could say that.'

The shopkeeper didn't know that Cook was in the police force, and Cook wanted to keep it that way. Mixing business with pleasure invariably spoiled both.

'I was reading the other day about one such lady,' said Cook. 'Maxine something-or-other. Got herself murdered.'

'Yes, I read about that too.'

'Was she a customer of yours?'

It was the sort of question that could lead to a lucky break, but having had one break already that day Cook wasn't too optimistic about a second. He was right.

'No. Wish she had been a customer. I might have got on the telly.'

Cook paid for the stick. 'Takes all sorts to make the world.'

'True. I hope they get the fellow who did it.'

'I expect they will.' Cook gave a little smile. 'The police are pretty good at that sort of thing.'

'They didn't do so well with the Yorkshire Ripper. It was luck he got caught.'

'We all need luck,' said Cook feelingly.

Back at headquarters he said, 'No developments while I was out?'

'The Super wanted you. Wanted to know where you were and I couldn't tell him. I got a rocket.'

'Bloody hell.' Cook knew his luck had run out. 'What did he want?'

'An update on the case.'

'Couldn't you tell him?'

'He wanted it from the horse's mouth.'

'When he gets on my back I feel like a pantomime horse, and the arse-end at that.'

Wilkins gave a sly look. 'Why don't you wave your magic stick and make him disappear?'

For an amazed moment Cook wondered if Wilkins knew of his visit to the store which sold props. But this was impossible. 'Did he want me to call him back?'

'No. In the end I think I satisfied him.'

'Anything else happen, apart from the Super?'

'No, but I've put a man on Samson's tail and arranged for a tap.'

'Fatty might be a good guy to some, but I'd like to nail him. Conspiracy to pervert the course of justice might be one of the hammers.'

★ ★ ★

100

The man who Cook wanted to nail knocked on the door of a house in a quiet part of London's West 8 district. In his hand he held a note ready to put through the letter-box if there was no answer to his knock.

The door opened. Phelan's frame filled the entrance. He frowned. 'What brings you here?'

'I've been trying to get you on the phone. No reply.'

'Not surprising. I've been out. Come in.'

Samson was taken into the sitting room with its bookcases containing the collected works of Karen Fitzwilliams. The french windows leading to the small walled garden were open. Phelan waved towards a long settee. 'Have a seat.' He switched off the radio which had been broadcasting light orchestral music. 'Have you turned up something?'

Samson eased his bulk on to the settee. 'Not much. I've found someone who's a bit of an expert on women like Maxine Eastbank. He's making a study of them. He tells me she was a supporter of animal welfare organisations and so there's no doubt in my mind that she was the one who put you in the cage, but I'm no nearer finding the other two. Oh, yes, and I know where your watch is. The police have it.'

'How the hell did they get it?'

Phelan had been standing casually, hands in pockets, near the french windows. His stance changed suddenly, hands came out of pockets and he looked poised for action.

'It was found beside the body. The police are very keen to locate its owner.'

Phelan swore in a mixture of English and Swahili and then said, 'I'm being set up for murder.'

'It does look like it,' said Samson. 'On the other hand, until you moved here your whereabouts were known to anyone wanting to frame you. It could have been done by making an anonymous phone call to the police and tipping them off.'

'So you don't think I'm being framed?'

'I'm keeping an open mind.'

Phelan walked across to a glass-topped table where a decanter of whisky stood by two glasses. He poured himself a measure. 'How about you? Like one?'

'Not at the moment. There's more to tell you. This morning two police detectives called on me. They'd got my name from the fellow I mentioned, the student, and they realise I'm acting for someone who has been involved with Maxine Eastbank in some way. They wanted your name. Of course I didn't tell them but I haven't endeared myself to them and it puts you at some risk. I'm fairly sure my phone will be tapped and that's why I'm here, to tell you not to contact me. I'll contact you if I have any news.'

'I love this bloody country. I wish to God I'd taken the next flight out to Nairobi as soon as I'd delivered the tigers.'

'Why didn't you?' asked Samson.

'Why didn't I? It's hard to say. There was someone I wanted to visit in Scotland for one thing. For another, I felt like having a taste of western civilisation for a change. I should have known better, and I was a bloody idiot to let myself get caught up with media interviews. But it was something different. Novelty.' He paused and in a quieter voice added, 'Yes, I should have known better. I've never liked big cities. I've probably travelled more than most men but I'm never comfortable in big cities. A fish out of water, I guess.' He went across to the french windows and looked out. 'I feel hemmed in. I like space. What space is there here? I'm walled in. I've swapped one cage for another.' He turned to Samson. 'I'm not asking for advice. I can make up my own mind. But if you've got any suggestions I'd like to hear them.'

'Do what you say you should have done in the first place. Get the next flight out to Nairobi.'

Phelan pondered the suggestion. His face was as grim as a rough afrormosia carving of a tribal deity. At length he said, 'I'm not going to run away. I've got a score to settle.'

'Then I suggest you lie low. Don't let anyone know where you are.'

Phelan tossed back his whisky. 'It's so bloody boring. I'd go mad if I stayed indoors.'

'The decision is yours, as you say.'

'Besides, as well as you, and the woman who comes in each day, there's someone else who knows I'm here.'

'Mr and Mrs Ormerod?'

'I wasn't thinking of them . . . Cindy.'

Samson's heavy eyelids rose fractionally. 'The Cindy who went with you to the TV studio? The one you think might be one of the trio?'

Phelan averted his gaze and seemed almost embarrassed. 'I

was mistaken about her. She's on my side.'

'Don't tell me you went to the bar where you met her and got picked up again.'

'It wasn't like that.' Phelan faced Samson. 'I decided I'd have a shot at finding her. I went to half the bars in the West End.'

'Not all in one night?'

'No.'

'You didn't tell me about this in the Eros bar,' said Samson reprovingly.

'I know. It was after I met you that day Cindy and I met, by accident, in the street. And she's not a whore. She didn't pick me up. She was, well, sort of playing around.' He hesitated. 'Just a game really.'

When tempted, Samson was not the sort of man to miss a chance of ironic comment. 'Oh, I see. Just a game. Does it have rules, this game? Can any number play?'

Anger sparked briefly in Phelan's eyes. He didn't care for the mocking tone of Samson's voice, but there was something about the detective he did like. Maybe it was the man's hippo quality; one could visualise Samson splashing around in the upper reaches of the Nile. 'Cut the sarcasm,' he said. 'Cindy is all right.'

'You trust her?'

'God, no. I wouldn't trust any woman. Any man, for that matter, unless I knew him very well indeed. No, I don't trust her. But she's all right.' He poured himself another whisky. 'Are you sure you won't join me?'

'Maybe a small one. Then I must be on my way.'

'I'm out of ice.'

'That doesn't matter.'

Phelan poured another whisky. 'You don't have to hurry. I'm fed up being cooped up and Cindy won't be here until six this evening at the earliest.' He handed Samson the drink. 'Cheers.'

Samson lifted the glass in acknowledgement. 'If Cindy isn't on the game, although she likes playing games, what does she do for a living? Or is she a woman of independent means, as they used to say?'

'She works for a firm of architects. A secretary. She was on an afternoon off to visit her dentist when I met her again. But she might be of help.'

'Oh? How?'

'One of her friends campaigns against companies which use animals in experiments for cosmetic products. Cindy will get this friend to find out what she can about similar groups.'

'Some would say it's all grist to the mill,' said Samson, echoing Cook's words earlier that day.

'What's your next move?'

'As I've told you, I don't normally discuss such things. I've made an exception with you so far. But my next move is something I'm keeping to myself.'

Phelan looked disgruntled. 'I hope you get somewhere soon. I want results. I'm not made of money.'

Samson drank his whisky and stood up. 'I want results too. I'm sure your friend Cindy wants to be helpful but has it occurred to you that her efforts might prejudice mine?'

'I don't follow.'

'If the guilty parties get wind of her enquiries it would put them on guard and make mine more difficult.' Samson moved towards the door. 'By the way, have you got yourself another watch?'

'Not yet.'

'I would, if I were you. And make it a used one. Something which you might have had for years. I'll be in touch.'

When he arrived back at his office Samson found two people waiting to see him; they were the parents of a teenage boy who was taking hard drugs and they wanted Samson to find out where he was obtaining supplies. He agreed to take on the case, but it was a long interview and some time before he was able to talk with Shandy. By now it was late afternoon and she brought him his customary cup of tea.

'Where are the biscuits?' he asked.

'There aren't any.'

'Why not?'

'I didn't buy any.' She flicked back a lock of hair from her forehead and gave a defiant look.

'Part of your campaign to persuade me to lose avoirdupoids?'

'That's right. I don't want a dead boss. Jobs aren't easy to get these days. Did you see Phelan?'

'Changing the subject from the unwelcome one of job-finding? Yes, he was in.' Samson gave a résumé of what had been said, and went on, 'I was followed. Someone's put a tail on me.'

'They know where he lives then?'

Samson smiled. 'No. I got the cabbie to drop me in Kensington High Street. A Rover 3500 pulled up behind and a guy got out. A physically fit man. I took my time paying the cabbie and this guy loitered. So I played a hunch and strolled down the street. He followed. I walked back and went into John Barker. Big stores are excellent places for losing tails.'

Shandy looked puzzled. 'Who?'

'It could be nothing to do with Phelan. He's not our only client, thank heavens, but my guess is that our CID friend, Cook, is behind it. I'm fairly sure everything said this morning was recorded. His sidekick had a briefcase which he half-opened and then left alone.' Samson gave his pink and white smile. 'It's comic. I was craftily running a tape and they were craftily running a tape and I expect we both knew the score. I shall have to be careful if there are any more meetings with Cook that I don't contradict anything I said this morning. I got the impression he didn't warm to me.'

'Amazing. And you so lovable.'

Samson ignored the crack. 'Have you found out anything about Nan Bellman?' he asked.

'I have, but it doesn't help. Last week was the last of her series. She's away on holiday. The Seychelles.'

'Is that all?'

'What more do you expect?'

Samson sighed. 'I'm not saying that today has been an especially bad day.' He took a sip of tea and winced. 'It's just that some days are worse than others. And now you've cut out the sugar.'

His self-pity was received without sympathy. 'Don't be negative. What's the next step?'

Samson pushed the tea away. 'My uncle would have called that drink physic.'

'Physic?'

'An archaic term for medicine. He lived in the past and liked archaic words.'

'The next step?'

'Well, we don't seem to be getting anywhere with the animal rights angle. There are too many organisations and splinter groups. It's as bad as the Church. There's the RSPCA cat and dog brigade, the anti-blood sports brigade, the anti-vivisection brigade, the anti-zoo brigade, the anti-ritual-slaughter brigade, the anti-culling brigade, the animal liberation brigade, the anti-performing animals brigade, the anti-battery hen brigade, and so on, and on. Somewhere among that lot, or just outside it, is a group committed to victimising people like Phelan who export animals, or perhaps it's simply an anti-export of white tigers brigade. By the time we've narrowed the field Phelan may be in deep trouble on a murder charge. So we must take a short cut.' He paused and looked up at Shandy. 'I'd like some sugar for that physic.'

'Oh, all right.' She left the room and returned with a bowl of sugar. 'How about switching to honey? It's much better for you.'

His eyes twinkled under their drooping lids. 'Honey for Samson? Out of the strong came forth sweetness? Very apt.'

'Not bad for an agnostic. . . . Now you've had your sugar, what did you mean when you said we must take a short cut?'

'A bit of housebreaking. I'm hoping Eastbank's house is more or less as she left it; hasn't been cleared out or reoccupied. I've no doubt she left an estate; probably quite a few assets. Her executor or administrator won't be in a position just yet to distribute the estate. The assets will be temporarily frozen. So I propose to go in and have a look around.'

'Won't you be too late? Won't the police already have done that and taken away anything of significance?'

Samson shook his head. 'They would only take away what they think is significant, stuff connected with her trade or profession. If they found stuff about animal welfare I doubt if they'd have taken it. No reason for them to. Not yet. But if they get on to Phelan then it could be very significant. So I need to remove any such clues and among any items I find and take there might be a clue for me.'

'The place might have burglar alarms.'

'It might, but what's the use of being a security expert if you don't know your way around security safeguards?' He stirred his cup of tea and took a sip. 'That's better.'

'When do you plan this break-in?'

'Tonight. Wish me luck.'

Her expression softened and she gave him a rare look of deep affection. 'Take care,' she said, 'I don't want to have to bring food parcels to jail.'

CHAPTER 13

'Detective Police Constable Horrocks, sir.'

Cook looked up from his desk at the young man standing in front of him. 'Hear you're the star of our football team, Horrocks. A striker.'

'A striker, sir. I don't know about star.'

'You like games with physical contact?'

'I don't mind them, sir.' The constable who had entered the room with a spring of confidence in his step looked a shade less self-assured. Why the hell was Cookie asking about sport, he wondered. He was soon to find out.

'A striker. Physical contact,' Cook mused. 'Pity you didn't strike today. I understand you lost contact.'

So this was it. Another example of Cook's awful humour. Fair enough. Now he knew where the goal-posts were he was ready to shoot, and he had something good to shoot.

'Yes, sir. He sussed out he was being followed and threw me off.'

'You made yourself too obtrusive.'

'With respect, I don't think so, sir. But he's a professional.'

'And so should you be, Horrocks.'

'I try to be, sir. I may have lost him but I've found out where he was going.'

'You found out where he was going?' Cook picked up a pencil and began twirling it between his fingers. 'How did you manage that?'

Horrocks flexed mental muscles. This was to be his shot at goal. Would Cook manage to deflect it?

'He was in a cab. The driver indicated that he was going to turn left down Victoria Road but then switched off his indicator and carried straight on for about fifty yards before pulling in by the kerb of Kensington High. Our man got out, paid his fare, taking his time, and wandered around a bit. He didn't look like someone who'd reached his destination. My guess was that he'd spotted he was being followed in the Rover and told his driver to drop him short of his objective.'

Cook nodded. 'A fair assumption. Go on.'

'As you say, sir, I lost him. But I'd already taken a note of the cab number, and I've followed that up. I've managed to have a word with the driver. He had been told to go to number 53 Ansdell Terrace which is less than a quarter of a mile from the spot where the fare was dropped off near John Barker's.'

Cook's lips had been tightly compressed but now they extended into what was intended as a smile but looked more like a hairline crack in his face. 'So all we want to know now is who lives at number 53 Ansdell Terrace. ... You might say that you scored after all, Horrocks.'

The young man responded by giving a smile to match Cook's. 'It's a striker's job to score, sir.'

'Have you followed it up?'

'Detective Sergeant Wilkins is doing so.'

'Good. Very good. All right, Horrocks. That's all.'

When the constable had left Cook lifted up the inter-phone. 'A word with you, Brian, if you're not too busy.'

'I'll be right in.'

A few moments later Detective Sergeant Wilkins was standing on the spot where Horrocks had stood. It was unusual for Cookie not to say, 'Have a seat.' Why was he to be kept standing? The trouble with Cookie was that you never quite knew where you were with him. One minute you were working together, shoulder to shoulder, and the next you were being given the cold shoulder.

'I won't keep you, Brian. Just one question. Why the hell wasn't I told about number 53 Ansdell Terrace? Why do I have to hear about it from a junior officer? And I wouldn't have heard if I hadn't sent for him because he'd lost Fatty Arbuckle.'

'Sorry about that.' When Cookie was being a pal you sometimes called him Desmond. When you were with others you called him 'sir'. Mostly you didn't call him anything, at least not aloud, although you called him names in your mind.

'Sorry? So you ought to be. I asked to be kept informed of all developments.'

'I know, but I wanted to present you with the full package,

108

not just the address, but the name of the occupant. Otherwise it would have been sort of half-cock.'

Cook forgave him with a smile and execrable humour. 'Half-cock, not to say, "Half-Cook". OK, I accept the explanation. You wanted to produce a rabbit out of a hat, didn't you, Brian? Well, leave that speciality to me in future. Right?'

'Right.'

'How's it going?'

'I've got a man working on it.'

'Let me know as soon as he gets a result. That's all.'

Cook worked late, periodically asking for progress reports. Everyone involved knew there would be no respite until he had a name. At last it came, brought by Wilkins.

'The house is owned by a Mr and Mrs Ormerod. They are in America. They've let someone called Phelan, Paul Phelan, occupy the house in their absence. A family friend, in a manner of speaking. Our informant thinks he was previously married to Mrs Ormerod. She's a writer and is in America with her husband.'

'Paul Phelan.' Cook spoke the name slowly as if savouring it. 'It doesn't ring any bells. Did you get this from a reliable source? . . . Oh, do take a seat, Brian.'

Wilkins moved across the room and sat down.

'Very reliable,' he said in answer to Cook's question. 'It was the housekeeper. A neighbour gave us her name and address.'

'And will tell Phelan she's done so.'

'I doubt it. The Ormerods aren't too popular. Although Mrs Ormerod is a celebrity, she won't mix.'

'So, who is this Paul Phelan? He's not on our list of punters. What does he do?'

Wilkins hesitated fractionally. He would have liked to take the whole credit for finding out Phelan's occupation but he knew Cook would have winkled out the truth and so it was better to be truthful from the start.

'Someone remembered seeing him on a television programme. He's an animal trader. He catches and exports wild animals. Sells them to zoos.'

'An unusual job. Who saw him on telly?'

'Detective Constable Horrocks.'

'Horrocks? He may have a future and not just in football.'

'Maybe.'

'And what else do we know about Phelan?'

'Not much. But we're in touch with Interpol.'

'Good. A fellow in that trade might have some sort of record. Anything else?'

'He has a woman friend. A Cindy Hardacre. She was his guest at the TV show and signed the visitors' book.'

Cook gave a wintry smile and said, 'Cindy Hardacre? Let's hope he doesn't get hard achers from her.'

Wilkins laughed. When Cook cracked his dreadful jokes it was best to encourage him. 'Hard achers! That's good.' And, apart from keeping Cookie happy, in CID work you needed jokes, however bad, to blunt the sharp edge of reality.

'What do we know of Cindy Hardacre?' asked Cook.

'Nothing.'

'She's not into this so-called domination scene?'

'Not so far as we know.'

Cook brooded for a few moments. 'That's a pity,' he said eventually. 'It would have tied up nicely. *Tied up* nicely.'

Wilkins gave another dutiful laugh. 'Tied up nicely. That's good.'

'Not really. Tell me, Brian, when the Eastbank house was searched there were some pamphlets and other bumf about animals, wasn't there?'

'There was.'

'Did we take it?'

'I don't think so. Not relevant to our enquiry.'

'It may have been relevant if this Phelan fellow makes a living from animals.'

'Right.'

'And so you know what we do?'

'Recover the bumf?'

'I don't think we need go through official procedures. It takes too long. Someone, Horrocks maybe, can use a bit of initiative, but make sure he doesn't wake up the neighbours by triggering a burglar alarm. And make sure he has back-up. OK?'

'Message received and understood.'

'Good. See to it, Brian.'

When Wilkins had left, Cook reached into a zipper bag and took out the magnetic-tipped stick. He proceeded to twirl it round his fingers making it dance back and forth along his knuckles. With familiarity the stick would become an extension of himself, another limb. While he practised the deft manipulation he thought with satisfaction of the progress to date. There were still three punters who had unsatisfactory alibis and would need to be leaned on, but instinct told him that Phelan was now the most likely suspect.

A man who traded in animals was the sort one would expect to have a crocodile leather strap on his wrist-watch. It remained a mystery why Maxine Eastbank had laid off her maid for three days before her death. Could it be that Phelan was a very special client, one for whom she made no record in her red book and she wanted to spend time with him?

Cook stopped twirling the stick and put it away. If Phelan could be indicted for murder, a certain private eye would have his fat nose rubbed in the dust. Obstructing the police in their enquiries was a very serious offence, particularly when the police were represented by himself, Detective Inspector Cook.

Obstruction of the police in the execution of their duties was another hammer he would use to nail Samson.

CHAPTER 14

Samson waited until dusk before reconnoitring the street where Maxine Eastbank had once lived. There was little road traffic and even fewer pedestrians. He passed a Jew whose head was bent over a book of scriptures and an old woman with an aged King Charles spaniel on a lead. When both were out of sight Samson surveyed the premises. He recognised the alarm box on the façade of the house as one of the less expensive systems which would be easy to neutralise. He moved on. In an hour's time, when it was dark, he would return with wire-cutters, a bunch of skeleton keys and wearing gloves.

It was an advantage that there were no houses on the other side of the street and, confident that no one in the row of Victorian villas would see him, Samson let himself in through the front door. He switched on a torch and moved down the hallway. When searching a house it was always best to start from the top and work downwards. In emergency the odds on escape were marginally weighted in favour of someone moving towards the ground rather than away from it.

The house had three storeys and he mounted two flights of stairs before coming to a small landing off which were three attic rooms. Two of these were bedrooms and Samson drew the curtains before scanning the rooms with masked torchlight. In each room the wardrobes were empty although he was intrigued by the interior of one wardrobe which had a pair of manacles fitted at shoulder height and another pair fitted close to the base. He hurriedly looked through chests of drawers but these only contained blankets, sheets and pillow cases, although in one drawer he found half a dozen baby's diapers, a card of safety pins and a box of rubber teats. The contents of all drawers were jumbled as though someone had already searched through them.

In the second bedroom what appeared to be a collapsible

112

child's cot was folded and resting against a wall which had been covered with wallpaper depicting characters from Walt Disney cartoons. The third room was completely empty and smelled musty. Bare floorboards creaked under his tread and he tiptoed out to the landing and down the stairs.

On the next floor he found a bathroom, a shower room and two bedrooms. The main bedroom was obviously the one which had been occupied by Maxine Eastbank. Jars of face cream and other cosmetics stood on the surface of a kidney-shaped dressing table and along the length of one wall a wardrobe with sliding mirror-fronted doors had been constructed. Samson eased back each door in turn and found rows of dresses and coats. One dress lay crumpled on the floor as if it had been pulled off a hanger. Trapped odours from the clothes mingled with a faintly musky scent which permeated the bedroom. Approximately thirty pairs of shoes and boots stood in regimental order on the wardrobe floor. Because he'd once had a client whose wife had hidden valuables in her boots Samson felt inside all the boots but they were empty.

He turned his attention to a couple of chests of drawers. These, as he expected, were filled with other items of clothing, some of it erotically fashioned, sheer and diaphanous. There were also laced corsets and other types of foundation garments, including a basque in pliant black leather. Torchlight illuminated a large double bed which was covered by a quilted silk overlay but its principal feature was a mirror bed-head shaped like an inverted heart. A television set which could be controlled from the bed stood in a far corner and a telephone rested on a bedside table. It was as the light swept past the television set that Samson saw something which froze him to the floor in shocked disbelief. A man's body was hanging from a crucifix.

Except for a loincloth the man was naked. His arms were spread apart and pinioned and his head lolled down. He was dreadfully dead. The shock receded as Samson noticed that on the lolling head was a crown of thorns. He was gazing at a life-size statue of Christ.

Having recovered from his shock Samson went to the other bedroom. It seemed to be a general purpose room. Although it had a bed there was also a typewriter on a table and an old-fashioned wooden filing cabinet decorated with scallop-shell motifs. He opened the drawers, beginning at the bottom and working towards the top, in the manner of a professional thief. It was obvious that, like all other drawers in the house, someone had turned over the stock. In each drawer papers were in a chaotic muddle. One drawer was completely empty and he guessed its contents had been extracted.

It was in the drawer next to the top that he found a mass of literature about animal welfare. He put down the torch and began taking the papers and stuffing them into a plastic carrier bag. When the bag was full he closed the drawer and opened the top drawer. It contained a jumble of holiday brochures.

Although he felt sure he had found what he sought, he decided to explore the ground floor. It was as he was walking through the entrance hall to the room where once Maxine Eastbank had allowed clients to wait that he heard a sound at the front door. A key was turning in the lock. He switched off the torch and backed towards the nearest door.

Out of the darkness he heard a man say, 'You wait here. I'll try upstairs.'

He edged backwards and his fingers felt the outline of another door. This must be the room from where special clients witnessed the suffering of others. If he went a little further he would reach the steps which led to the basement. He could hide there until the other housebreakers, whoever they were, had gone.

Very gingerly, feeling for each step with his foot, he descended into a chilly chamber. Above, there was absolute silence. He switched on the torch again. Light illuminated a cage. He swept the beam around the chamber. Someone had removed whips and other gear but the rack was still in place.

So this was where Phelan had been trapped. For the first time Samson began to understand his client's obsessive desire for revenge. He switched off the torch. It was unlikely that the other housebreakers would look for loot in a basement. He'd give them half an hour and then cautiously ascend.

From time to time he flashed the torch on his watch. The minutes passed slowly. He thought about the men above, he thought about his flat and wished he was in bed, he thought about his office, he thought of Shandy, and he thought of the place where he was hiding. How could anyone pay to be incarcerated here? And be physically maltreated? The theories of Simon Jones seemed naively simplistic. It wasn't the guilt complexes of wicked capitalists that drove men to excesses, it must be something buried very deep in the human psyche. He had long since ceased to be surprised by the vagaries of human nature. One just had to accept that different people had different drives and for every theory and rule there were so many exceptions as to make theories and rules worthless.

He glanced at his watch once more and was about to make his way up the steps when he heard sounds.

A man's voice said, 'Do you want to see the chamber of horrors?'

'Not half. I was going to ask.'

'All part of your education, Bob.'

Samson stepped sideways and crouched under the stairway. The sound of footsteps as the two men descended echoed round the basement. Samson gripped his torch tightly as light from another torch swept round the bare walls.

'It's a pity her Mum and Dad had some of the apparatus removed,' said the first man. 'They're going to have a job getting the cage out. It must have been assembled on the spot. Custom built.'

The other man laughed nervously. 'It would give me the creeps to be stuck in here.'

They had reached the bottom of the stairs and were close to Samson.

'Imagine spending a night here.'

'No, thanks.'

'Cookie reckons she was worth a packet. Crime doesn't pay but perversion does.'

Light lingered on the rack and the man who was shining the torch moved forward. The beam swept around and Samson knew that discovery was one second away. He moved fast.

With his torch he hit the wrist of the torch-holder hard. The man cried out in pain and Samson switched on his own torch and shone it straight into the face of the other man who, temporarily blinded, tried to shield his eyes. As his arm came up Samson kicked him in the groin. Then he swung his torch to hit the first man on the head. Having temporarily disabled both men Samson ran up the stairs. He slammed the door at the top, ran down the hall, wrenched open the front door, and sped out into the night.

A car was parked near a street lamp and a man was sitting

behind its wheel. Samson turned smartly and hurried away in the opposite direction but when he heard a shout – 'Get after him!' – he began running.

Suddenly he was caught in headlights. The car engine started and the doors slammed. He turned a corner and almost at once came to a narrow alleyway which passed behind the row of villas. He darted down it just as the car turned the corner. It raced off down a side street. Moments later Samson heard the squeal of its brakes but he had recovered his breath sufficiently to hurry to the end of the alleyway. He turned left and was soon in a main thoroughfare where he flagged down a taxi. Within half an hour he was back in the safety of his flat.

After emptying the plastic bag of the papers he had taken he looked through pamphlets about cruelty to animals and saw some grisly photographs of emaciated dogs and terrified monkeys. But what gripped his attention was a cyclostyled paper headed 'Operation White Tigers'.

The paper contained instructions for a gathering of members outside Shepherd's Bush Post Office and stated, 'a decoy will lure the target towards you. You will crowd around to protect the decoy while the target is dealt with. He will be taken to Maxine's and given the treatment he deserves. This will continue until he signs a declaration renouncing his loathsome trade.' The paper was signed, 'Pam and Cynth'.

Fine, thought Samson, I've only got to find two women called Pam and Cynthia.

He went through more papers and then came across a letter with an address heading in Streatham. It went:

Dear Maxine,
    The flowers were a lovely surprise. Yes, I should like to join you on holiday in October. I think we have a lot in common apart from a love of animals. To hell with men!
                                                            Love,
                                                            Pam

Samson put down the letter and went to a small kitchen. He was feeling very hungry. Shandy wouldn't approve but he intended increasing his cholesterol level. Two eggs and some rashers of smoked back bacon should do the trick. His appetite was sharpened by the knowledge that he had foiled men belonging to

116

Detective Inspector Cook's squad. As the bacon sizzled he sung softly to himself, 'Lookie, lookie, lookie, here comes Cookie, walking down the street; lookie, lookie, lookie, here comes Cookie, ain't she sweet.'

That night he slept well and woke shortly after seven with rain pattering against the window pane. The warm, dry Indian summer had ended.

He was at his office a few minutes before Shandy. Her face registered surprise. 'Couldn't you sleep?' she asked.

'I slept like a top.'

'How did it go last night? I expected to get a call to tell me.' She gave a rueful smile. 'So while I was worrying about you, you were sleeping like a top.'

'At least one of us had a good night,' said Samson, and before she could reply he went on to tell her of the episode in Maxine Eastbank's house.

As he spoke, Shandy took off her raincoat and put out an umbrella to dry. Then she sat at her desk while Samson continued his narrative, detailing the room by room search. When he came to the shock of seeing the realistic sculpture of a man hanging on a cross she said, 'What an amazing thing to find in a brothel boudoir.'

'I thought the same at first. But is it so amazing that a professional dominatrix should like to have the statue of a man in a particularly cruel form of bondage in her bedroom? Perhaps the amazing thing is that so many people who would be revolted at the idea of bizarre sex are quite happy to kneel before such a statue and worship.'

'Let's not get into a religious argument. What happened next?'

Her eyes widened when he told her of the other intruders and how he had made his escape and been chased.

'I was right to worry about you,' she said. 'Do you think they'll know it was you?'

'Cook will put two and two together and I'd guess his simple arithmetic is just about up to making four. But nobody got a sight of my face and anyone who says he did is a liar.'

'I'm not surprised you slept like a top. All that healthy exercise.'

'I must have lost a couple of pounds.'

She looked at his waistline, smiled and said nothing.

'So,' he said, 'now that you're here I'm off to Streatham.'

'Streatham? Why?'

'That's the end of the story. I went through the papers and this is what I found.' He produced the cyclostyled sheet and handwritten letter.

'Would you copy these for me to take? Keep the originals here.'

Shandy read the papers before photocopying them. As she handed him the copies she said, 'Good luck, take care, and don't end up in a cage.'

CHAPTER 15

'So you scored an own goal, Horrocks?'

'I wouldn't put it like that, sir.'

'How would you put it?'

The young constable braced himself. Cookie was in one of his moods. 'There was no evidence of another person in the house,' he said. 'He had the advantage of the element of surprise.'

'But you got a look at him? You'd recognise him if you saw him again?'

Horrocks shifted from one leg to the other. 'It could have been Mr Samson, sir, but I wouldn't want to swear to it.'

'I'm sure it was Fatty Arbuckle. No prints?'

'None, sir. He was wearing gloves.'

'And no sign of bumf about our dumb friends?'

'It had been taken. We were a few minutes too late.'

Cook picked up a pencil from his desk and began twirling it between his fingers.

'What I can't understand is why the two of you went into the basement. You didn't think the bumf had flown itself there, did you?'

'No, sir.'

'Not been wafted there on a gentle breeze?'

'No, sir.'

'Not been transported by a genie on a magic carpet?'

'No, sir.'

'Then what the hell was the point of going down?'

Horrocks was visibly embarrassed. 'Constable Beecham is new to the job. I thought it might be educational for him. Get an idea of the seamy side of life.'

'Educational? You and Beecham were both educated in the art of surprise by Fatty.'

With a deft flick the pencil shot out of Cook's fingers and hit the unsuspecting Horrocks on the chest. Stepping back involuntarily he almost lost his balance.

'Surprise can come from any quarter,' said Cook. 'Always be on guard against surprise. Pick up my pencil, will you?'

Horrocks obeyed and handed the pencil back to Cook who recommenced twirling it. After stepping away Horrocks stood a little further back than he had previously. He wasn't going to be caught again by a silly party trick.

'But all is not lost,' Cook continued. 'We are getting somewhere. We know Fatty has Phelan as a client. We also know that this Phelan brought two white tigers into the country. The Hilton has confirmed he wasn't using his room or the hotel's facilities for three days, two of which are not accounted for in Eastbank's life. We know Eastbank had connections with animal rights nutters, although thanks to Fatty slipping between your fingers, just like a pencil slipped between mine, we have no hard evidence of connections. We know a man hitched a lift from a spot near where Eastbank's body was found and we know that on the following morning Phelan returned to his hotel looking as though he'd been pulled through a hedge backwards. What we need now is a photo of Phelan. There should be plenty around. Try the PA library but don't go about it officially. We don't want the press hanging round again. . . . Why do you think I want a photo, Horrocks?'

The reply was instant. 'So it can be shown to the guy who gave the lift, sir. See if he can identify Phelan as his customer.'

'Correct. See to it then. And ask Sergeant Wilkins if he could spare a moment.'

After he had left the room Cook stretched his arms and yawned. Unlike Samson, he had slept badly, but insomnia was normal when he became deeply involved in a case, as he was in this one, not merely because he wanted a murder solved but he wanted to win the duel with Samson. It was almost as important to him to score off the private detective as it was to pin a murder charge on somebody, and if that somebody was Samson's client his cup would be full and proper sleep patterns restored.

A light tap on the door and Wilkins entered.

'Sit down, Brian.'

Wilkins complied with alacrity, glad he hadn't been summoned to be carpeted. Cookie had arrived in a bad mood but young Horrocks had somehow managed to mellow him a little.

'I've asked Horrocks to obtain a photo of Phelan. We'll see if what's-his-name, Stubbs, can identify him.'

'It'd be great if he could.'

'It would, but I'm getting pessimistic about identification procedures. They're loaded in favour of villains. Apart from that, I don't think Stubbs wants to be involved. He'll say he can't be sure. But we'll try it. But assuming that we aren't lucky, what's our next step?'

'We'll watch Phelan's movements. Check out all his contacts. I can get a man on it.'

'It'll have to be a good man. Phelan makes a living trapping animals. He's an experienced tracker and good trackers know when they're being tracked. We aren't dealing with a City gent. And Fatty has probably warned him we're in the hunt.'

'Right.'

'I'd like to know if he wears a watch and, if so, whether it's a new one or one he's had some time.' Cook's face cracked. 'Some time.' He waited for Wilkins's smile, appreciative of the word play, before going on, 'But the operation mustn't be prejudiced on account of this. The watch isn't as crucial as it was. Anything from Interpol yet?'

'Not yet. But I'm waiting for a call from a pal in the Belgian Sûreté.'

'Has this pal got pull?'

'No pull, but he started his career in the Mission de Burundi pour l'Europe in Brussels.'

'That explains everything,' said Cook. 'I don't know why I was so stupid to ask. But perhaps you'd be so kind as to tell me what working in some mission implies.'

Wilkins had done some solid groundwork and wasn't thrown by Cook's sarcasm.

'I've been through all the newspaper cuttings on Phelan and the white tigers, including a useful review of the TV interview. It's only in the last few years he's been a trapper. Before that he was a dealer in animal skins and he operated mostly in Burundi which, as I'm sure you'll know, is a small republic in the middle of Africa. Before its independence it was part of Belgian territory called Ruanda-Urundi. Phelan was there around the time my pal was in the Mission and it struck me he might know something which isn't in Interpol records. It's a long shot, but worth a try, I thought.'

Cook evaluated the long shot. 'Worth a try,' he admitted, 'let me know how it goes. And remember, I want to be kept informed of all developments. No more waiting until you've got a "full package". . . . Still no record that Phelan was one of Eastbank's clients?'

'No.'

'I'll bet he and Eastbank spent two days together. It fits so nicely. The bits are falling into place. What we need is a clincher and then we'll move in and have a little talk with Mr Phelan and give Fatty a kick up the arse. OK, Brian, that's all.'

Wilkins turned to leave and the moment his back was to Cook an expression of satisfaction stole across his face. His voice had been flat and his eyes blank when he'd given Cook a brief lesson on the status of Burundi but his 'as I'm sure you'll know' was intentionally condescending and in retaliation for Cook's sarcasm.

He was even more satisfied to return within the hour to say, 'I've heard from my pal in Brussels.'

'And?' enquired Cook.

'He had heard of Phelan. Quite interesting. Nothing was ever proved but most whites in the community in Usumbura – that's the capital, it's now called Bujumbura, and it's on the northern tip of Lake Tanganyika . . .'

'Get on with it,' interrupted Cook.

'He killed a Belgian called Verhaeren. Said it was a shooting accident and the only witness was his gun-bearer. But he and Verhaeren were enemies and nobody was surprised when one was shot by the other.'

'Wasn't he tried?'

'No. There was a judicial enquiry but the verdict was accidental death. My pal remembers the case quite clearly. A report came through on the Telex in his office.'

The satisfaction on Wilkins's face spread across the room to Cook.

'Nice work, Brian. Very useful. It establishes he's a killer. Once a man is a killer he's potentially always a killer. It's the first killing that's the most difficult. I'm more than ever sure Phelan is our man. But we'll keep going with the other punters.'

'We've got a photo of Phelan,' said Wilkins. 'Shall I try it on Stubbs?'

'Yes, and if you have any luck let me know at once, but my

bet is still he won't commit himself.'

Cook proved to be right. The mini-cab driver refused to make a positive identification.

'The only thing he was clear about,' said Wilkins in disgust, 'is that blue safari suit. I've checked with the hotel receptionist who saw Phelan come back after being away for three days and she can't remember what he was wearing. She only remembers he looked tired and hadn't shaved.'

'Never mind,' said Cook. 'We've got him in our sights.'

CHAPTER 16

For a while after Samson's visit Phelan sat pondering what the detective had said. It was disquieting that the police seemed to be following a trail which could lead to him but he felt certain he hadn't killed Maxine Eastbank while under the influence of a drug and, as yet, wasn't unduly worried. As for Samson's suggestion that if Cindy started making her own enquiries it might make his job more difficult, Phelan decided he'd tell her to hold back for the time being.

Resentful of feeling cooped up, and being at a loose end, he looked along the shelves of books written by Karen. Each book had run into many editions. In his own words Phelan wasn't a great reader but he had about three hours to pass before he could expect to see Cindy. She had left him at nine that morning, smiling brightly and saying, 'Hopefully, I'll be back by six. I'll give you a call if I'm likely to be later.'

He picked out one or two books at random, leafed through them and put them back, and then he came to a book which was an account of her travels through Africa. The book came open at a chapter headed, 'Night in a Native Hut'. The first sentence ran: 'Paul Freeling was a dealer in animal hides and skins whom I met by chance when trying to buy a leopard skin from a street trader in Usumbura. . . .'

Phelan couldn't have been more astonished if a leopard had suddenly appeared by his side. He poured another drink and read on. The book related how Paul Freeling and Karen, travelling on a rough track between Usumbura and Kitega, had been stopped by a landslide. The headman of a nearby village had offered hospitality and, after eating, the villagers had danced to the rhythm of drums. She had been given a native hut for her sleeping quarters and, of what followed, she had written, 'Paul Freeling stayed on guard outside my hut all night long and I was immensely grateful for his protection.'

He tossed the book to one side. Not only had she given him a false name, and not had the nerve to tell the truth about their night together in the hut, she had implied, as she had throughout the chapter, that she could have been in danger from the Bahutu villagers but for the presence of her protector, Paul Freeling. This was an insult to a peaceful and welcoming people.

After a while he picked up the book and resumed reading, not for entertainment, or to find fault with her colourful exaggerations, but to see if she had mentioned Verhaeren. Although a feud had existed between the two men before she came to Burundi, she had exacerbated it by accepting Verhaeren's hospitality while he, Phelan, was away buying hides. But his rival appeared in only one paragraph and then as a heavy-drinking Belgian.

It was almost six o'clock when he put down the book. Cindy would soon be back and he'd promised to prepare a meal. Having eaten out so much recently he was looking forward to the evening ahead and planned to start the meal with avocado and prawns, purchased that morning, and this would be followed by lamb chops, petits pois and potato croquettes. They'd finish with cheese and fruit. When Cindy arrived back from work they'd have a drink, eat the meal at leisure, maybe watch a film on video – Karen had a small library of video cassettes – and then go to bed. For the time being, he'd follow Samson's advice and lie low.

When she hadn't arrived by seven he grew restless. Patience, like passivity, was not one of his characteristics. He went out of the front door and looked down the short, narrow street which branched in three directions at the end. There were plenty of parked cars but apart from a man at the end of the street who was adjusting a car aerial there was no one to be seen. He went indoors again.

A wall clock showed the time at seven twenty-five. He had lost the habit of glancing at his wrist but still found the absence of a watch irksome. Seven thirty. He went outside again and looked down the street. A woman was unloading late shopping from her car and, at the end of the street, the man who had been fiddling with the aerial was now examining a box in his hand. It looked as if it might be the car's radio. Phelan went indoors again. He was growing angry. Why the hell hadn't she given

125

him a call as promised?

He looked at the pink prawns lying in their pale green bower and at the lamb chops waiting to be grilled and he began to feel hungry. If she hadn't arrived by eight, he'd eat on his own.

Eight o'clock came and went. He prepared and doggedly ate the meal although he had now lost his appetite for food, but not for drink. By nine thirty, having given her up, he was half-drunk and bored. He gazed at a near empty bottle of Chivas Regal and wished for the hundredth time he'd never come to London. It was a lousy, dirty, stinking place filled with lousy, dirty, stinking people. He was hit by a wave of maudlin nostalgia; maybe Samson had been right and he should get out, take the next flight to Nairobi. He reached for the bottle, gripped it clumsily and spilled some whisky on the surface of the glass-topped side table. 'Shit,' he said aloud. He couldn't be bothered to wipe up the little pool of liquid.

Ten o'clock, and he decided that if Cindy should turn up now she could spend the night on the doorstep. He stood up unsteadily and staggered out of the room and up the stairs to a bathroom. Even out in the wild, with a scarcity of water, he had never failed to clean his teeth before turning in for the night.

Five minutes later he was sprawled across a bed deep in sleep.

It may have been on account of unresolved resentment against Cindy, or through memories stirred by Karen's book, but it was a bad night for dreams. He was once again being taunted by Verhaeren to fire, just as he had been taunted in waking life many years before, when he'd been told that if he hadn't the guts to pull the trigger Verhaeren would come openly for Karen. In the dream, he fired, but only a cork popped out and Verhaeren began mocking him in a tongue which became Kirundi and it was Murunga speaking. '*Uko zivugijive niko zitambura*' – 'one dances to the rhythm of the drums,' a saying used by natives when talking of submission to authority. Murunga, friend and gun-bearer, was telling him to submit to Verhaeren. But Verhaeren had changed into his father who was sadly waving him farewell as he left on the train from Freetown and in no time he was standing alone on an unfamiliar plateau. Verhaeren stepped out from behind some bushes, laughing and pointing at him. . . .

He went through a cycle of dreams in which Verhaeren,

126

Murunga and his father kept changing places, and all the time he was travelling, trying to find Karen. He finally awoke, exhausted, with another of Murunga's favourite sayings running like a repetitive tune through his mind. '*Ingego ntipfa hapfa nyeneyo,*' which translated meant, 'a habit doesn't die, but the one who has it does'.

For a while he lay awake staring at the ceiling and then he turned on his side and within seconds had fallen into mercifully dreamless sleep. When he awoke for the second time it was almost nine o'clock. He got up, showered and shaved, and went downstairs. A letter lay on the front door mat. He picked it up. The envelope had a London postmark. He didn't recognise the handwriting. Who knew he was here? Who had found him? He tore open the envelope and went straight to the end, to the signature. It was 'Cindy' and above was the single word, 'Sorry.'

Dear Paul

I think you deserve an explanation. It's not easy to give you one. I suppose it's a mixture of things. But first, don't try to find me again. You won't. I'm staying with a friend. Incidentally, I don't work for a firm of architects. I have a rather humdrum job. I'm an ordinary working woman.

I feel bad about letting you down because you confided in me but I can promise you that what you told me won't be related elsewhere and I shan't tell anyone where you're living.

To be honest, your personality came over a bit too strong for me. Your obsession with finding and punishing the people who trapped you was rather frightening. I can understand how you felt but it was the way you kept returning to the subject. You couldn't let it go. Once or twice I felt quite scared. You were different from the man who stayed in my flat and took me to the TV studio.

I would hate you ever to have a grudge against me. I know you must have one, but it can only be a small one, but if I saw much more of you and then did something you didn't like, I'd be really worried.

I don't expect you'll understand, Paul, it's not so much you as a person as a sort of force inside you, if that makes sense. Perhaps none of this will make sense to you. I'll close wishing you all the best, and saying,

Sorry,
Cindy

Phelan read the letter with a sort of disbelief. What did she mean – 'the way you kept returning to the subject'? He'd scarcely mentioned his ordeal or his intention to exact full punishment. And why the hell should she find him frightening? He might not be the most polished companion but he had behaved well. And if she was so frightened, why had she gone to bed with him? Was she one of those women who got a kick out of sex with a man who simultaneously frightened and excited them?

She wrote of his obsession. Hadn't Karen said much the same thing years ago in Burundi? She'd called his hatred of Verhaeren obsessive. He put the letter away and went to the kitchen to make coffee.

Why should a natural desire for revenge be called obsessive? Was it what Cindy called the 'sort of force' inside him? Phelan wasn't given to self-analysis but he found it difficult to avoid these questions which sprang into his mind with the same repetitive compulsion as Murunga's sayings.

A habit doesn't die, but the one who has it does.

He knew he was habitually stubborn, but he wasn't habitually vindictive; he only wanted retribution when natural justice demanded it.

He found himself thinking of Isabella, his black mistress. She had once said, speaking of Verhaeren, 'You and he were too much alike in many ways.' And, after the shooting, he had degenerated as Verhaeren had, years before, by neglecting his business, drinking too much, cutting his European friends and going native.

Since the direction of his life had changed and he had earned a living by trapping and selling wild animals he had lost touch with Isabella. This was to be expected. She couldn't read or write, and she'd never been more than fifteen kilometres from Usumbura in her life. Suddenly he had a desire to see her again. She would have understood his wish for revenge and supported him. He'd never forgotten how she had reacted when someone had stolen one of her chickens. She had disappeared for three days and when she returned it was with the cooked remains of a dead chicken and the news that the thief was now in hospital having blood transfusions.

He looked outside. It was raining and the small segment of sky which could be seen was leaden grey. If he stayed here much longer he would certainly develop an obsessive hatred of London.

A habit doesn't die, but the one who has it does.

He went to the cloakroom and borrowed one of Dennis Ormerod's raincoats. Outside, he strode down the narrow street. With any luck, he'd pick up a taxi in Kensington High Street.

To his surprise the car with the aerial was still at the end of the street but a different man was sitting at the wheel. He was reading a newspaper. This could only mean that a watch was being kept on him. He rapped on the car window.

The man wound it down.

'If I see you again,' said Phelan with controlled menace, 'I'll break your bloody neck.'

The man gave him a peculiarly dead look which Phelan recognised. He'd seen that look before in men's eyes. They were men who weren't thrown by threats and could themselves intimidate with deadly meaning. Mercenaries often had this look in their eyes and so did policemen on tough assignments.

Instead of taking a taxi, which might be followed, Phelan hurried to the underground station. Once past the ticket barrier he paused and waited. He hadn't been followed by the man he'd threatened. After going by Tube to Victoria he hired a taxi to take him to Samson's office.

He was sick of London and, in a way, sick of himself. Maybe he was being ruled by an obsession. All right, he'd kick it. He'd tell Samson to drop the case, pay his fees, and disappear.

The rain had stopped by the time he arrived at Samson's office and the sidewalks glistened in light from the sun which had speared a hole in cloud cover. He went through a narrow entrance and up a flight of steps.

Shandy looked up from a typewriter as he walked in.

'I'd like to see your boss,' Phelan said.

She stood up and patted her hair. 'I'm sorry, you can't. Mr Samson isn't in.'

'When will he be back?'

'I don't know. Can I give him a message?'

'I've come to pay him off. Maybe you could give me the bill.'

'That's not possible. I can't make out a bill without his authority.'

'And you have to dance to the rhythm of the drums?'

She raised her eyebrows. 'If that means what I think it means, yes, I do.'

'Fair enough. Then he'll have to forward his account to me, care of Box 378, Express Services, Nairobi.'

'You're leaving us?'

'Urgent business commitment,' he said. It was a lie, and he didn't like lying, but he wasn't going to say, 'Maybe I stand more to lose than to gain by trying to settle scores.'

'That's a pity,' she said, 'because Mr Samson is away on your case. We have a very good lead.'

His hunting instincts were alerted. 'What is it?'

Shandy hesitated, uncertain whether Samson would approve of her divulging his movements. 'I can only say it's a very good lead.'

'Come on. I'm your client. I'm entitled to know what's going on.'

'You're pressurising me.'

'Sure I am. You dance to the rhythm of his drums when it comes to making out bills, but to my rhythm when it comes to information I'm paying for. What is this good lead?'

She gave him a cool look but he remained unchilled.

'If you're going back to Africa, does it matter?' she asked.

'Yes.'

'All right then. He thinks he knows the first names of the two women and the address where one lives. He's gone to check it out.'

'How did he find that out?'

'He *is* a detective. It's what you're paying him for.'

Phelan liked her crisp response, and the way she looked him in the eye. And the hunter in him, desiring to be in at the kill or the capture, was beginning to chase away introspective thoughts.

'Maybe I'll be able to hang on another day. Do you think he'll have it wrapped up by then?'

Shandy wrinkled her brow. 'That's a difficult question. He might. I can't say more than that.' She continued to look unwaveringly at him. 'I don't know anything about your business commitments, but it might be wise not to hang around too long in Britain.'

'I realise that. The goons are watching me. But I threw them off the scent. Anyone would think I'm suspected of murder.'

'Anyone would,' she agreed.

'You don't?'

'I think you might be suspected, yes.'

'I'm getting really browned off with this country,' said Phelan, 'but tell your boss I'm staying on one more day, and I'm expecting him to call me. And tell him that when I leave here I'm going to get myself a watch. Is there anywhere near here that sells good used watches?'

'You could try the street market. Turn left when you leave here and take the passage first left. It goes into a pedestrian precinct where there's a market.'

'Thanks. I'll be on my way.'

When the door closed after him, Shandy slumped slightly in her seat and said a soft, 'Phew!'

Phelan followed her directions and was soon in an area lined with the stalls of market traders. The place was alive with noise and movement, and the air filled with odours from a hot-dog stand which clashed with the smell of fish from a nearby stall. Fruit, cheap clothes and women's perfumes added to the conglomerate smell, and Phelan was momentarily reminded of an African market. It didn't create another wave of nostalgia, but he felt a ripple.

One stall was loaded with second-hand cutlery, bric-à-brac, clocks and watches. After examining a tray of second-hand watches Phelan selected a Timex which was in working order. It would serve its purpose until either he recovered his own watch or purchased a new one. He paid for it and strapped it on his wrist.

Unnoticed by him, a man in a T-shirt, leather blouson and jeans, moved from a stall selling electrical goods and went to the stall where Phelan had purchased the watch. He gave the stall-holder a brief glance at his identity card and asked the make of watch and how much had been paid for it.

CHAPTER 17

When Phelan had disappeared round a corner on his way to Samson's office, the man with a peculiarly dead look in his eyes used a transmitter in the car to call up a uniformed policeman with a walkie-talkie. The policeman acknowledged the message and went across to a shop doorway where a young man wearing a leather blouson and jeans was sheltering from the rain.

'He's on his way, moving in this direction, on foot, and in a hurry,' said the policeman.

'Right.'

The young man left the doorway and drifted down the street. Within a minute he had sighted Phelan. It wasn't difficult to follow by Tube and cab until Phelan went into Samson's office. After paying the cab driver the young man wandered down the street apparently window-shopping but keeping observation on the entrance to Samson's office. It was while he was gazing in the window of a shop which sold glass and chinaware that in the window's reflection he saw a face he recognised. He turned. 'Tony, what are you doing here?'

The other man, older, in a shabby grey suit and open-necked shirt, sounded depressed when he replied, 'Harry Horrocks has been pulled out and I've been drafted in, but I think the bugger must have given me the slip.'

'Never mind. He gave Harry the slip too.'

'I've been doing a recce,' said the older man, 'and there's a way out of his office at the back, down a fire escape. I reckon he uses it when he wants to do a flit.'

'I'll move on but we'll keep in contact. You never know, there might be room for us both on this.'

He was right. While he was checking with the stall-holder on Phelan's purchase, the older man took over as tail and followed Phelan, leaving the other to watch Samson's premises.

By switching roles they minimised the chances of Phelan suspecting he was being followed.

When Phelan had been trailed to his base, a report was radioed to headquarters by the man with the dead-looking eyes who had been cruising slowly round the block since alerting the uniformed policeman on Phelan's movements.

At headquarters Cook was listening to Wilkins who could barely keep a note of triumph from his voice or smugness from his face.

'I think I've persuaded our friend, Stubbs, to have a change of mind.'

Cook picked up a pencil. 'How did you manage that?'

'I paid an off-the-record visit. Just for a friendly chat. His wife was there. Not a bad looker. About five months gone, I'd say. She was a help. Reminded her old man how the guy who had an alleged broken-down Saab had been insulting about her delicate condition. How he'd said that expecting a baby wasn't a happy ending to a romance but bloody awful.'

Cook gave his thin smile. 'What a nasty thing to say.'

'Thoughtless.'

'Tactless.'

'What you'd expect from a man who incarcerates rare animals.'

'You're right, Brian. We're dealing with a man who lacks decent feelings.'

A grin spread across Wilkins's face. He was glad Cook was in a good mood. Shortly the mood should be even better.

'To cut a long story short, Brian, are you going to tell me Stubbs has changed his mind and thinks he can identify Phelan?'

'In a manner of speaking, yes.'

'A manner of speaking.' The pencil began to twirl between Cook's fingers. 'What exactly do you mean by that?'

Wilkins's confident demeanour slipped slightly. 'He still says he can't make a visual identification. He was mugged last year by a customer and says he'll never go on an identification parade again.'

'Why not?'

'He picked the wrong man and felt a right Charlie.'

The pencil raced along Cook's fingers as if frantically searching for paper.

'So what sort of identification did he make?'

'He's sure he could recognise the voice.'

'That won't be acceptable in a court as primary evidence.'

'No, but if he could make a positive voice identification it could help to break Phelan down, weaken his resistance, put more pressure on him.'

The inter-phone rang. Cook put down his pencil and answered it. He listened intently and when he put down the phone he said, 'That's a bit of good news, Brian. Another pointer in the right direction. Phelan has bought himself a watch from a market stall after visiting Fatty's office. Pity we don't know what Fatty himself is up to.' Cook stood up. 'I think it's time we paid Mr Phelan a visit.'

Wilkins looked uncertain. 'What sort of line are you going to take? He's bound to deny any connection with Eastbank and he'll have some excuse for being on the Epping road even if we can get him to admit he was there.'

'I'm surprised you should say that, Brian. We've got Eastbank's little red book with names and addresses of punters, haven't we?'

'Yes, but his name isn't in it.'

Cook frowned. 'That's funny. I could have sworn I saw it there. And the address of his hotel and room number.'

Realisation dawned on Wilkins's face. 'Can't think how I overlooked it.'

'Don't blame yourself, Brian. After all, it was in invisible ink. . . . Can someone oblige?'

Wilkins thought. 'John King is a bit of an artist.'

'King?'

'A constable seconded from "S" division.'

'Paints like a Constable, does he?'

The pun was lost on Wilkins. 'Yes, he paints. But I reckon he could do a fair copy of Eastbank's handwriting.'

'How could you say such a thing!' Cook sounded shocked. 'That would be tampering with evidence, not to say forgery. I don't want to hear any more about it. Be with me in half an hour, and we'll pay a call on Phelan. Oh, and bring that address book with you.'

When he returned after the visit to Samson's office Phelan found the housekeeper Hoovering the sitting room carpet. She had let herself in during his absence. He had forgotten that she might be there and found her presence and the hum of the vacuum cleaner

134

very irritating. He wanted to be alone to think in peace.

He went outside and sat in the small garden. The sky had cleared but the sun couldn't reach the garden and he sat in shade. This was another minor irritation. He missed the sun and warmth of Africa and the reliability of the weather. In England it could be oppressively humid one day and the next you could be shivering with cold; in the part of Africa he knew best there were dry seasons and rainy seasons and you could predict when they would come and go.

Ever since he had delivered the white tigers, and agreed to a television interview, things had gone wrong. Nobody believed he was a conservationist and in countless anonymous letters he had been called a cowardly thief. He had been humiliated by three nutty women, he had been taken for a ride by a silly little cow who had the nerve to tell him he was frightening and obsessive, he had been spied on, he was stuck in a sunless house, he was bored in mind and frustrated in spirit. Why not go back to where he belonged?

He waited impatiently for the housekeeper to leave and, when she did, he looked up the number for British Airways and booked a flight to Nairobi on the following day. Having accomplished this, his spirit was no longer frustrated, and his mind was at peace. To hell with London. He'd never come here again. As for Karen, he'd leave her a note of thanks. He didn't despise dream interpretations – witch-doctors were every bit as accurate in their interpretations as western psychoanalysts – and he knew from dreams that whatever he might think when he was awake, his sleeping self was still searching for the love he thought he had found in her and the home he'd hoped they would make together. But in dreams, and sometimes in waking moments, he thought of Isabella too. Was she still in Usumbura, now Bujumbura?

He remembered how every day when he arrived in his car at the warehouse where skins were cured he would drive straight at the women working in the yard and they would scatter like pigeons, shrilling with laughter. But one woman never moved. She would stand firm and he'd had to brake violently more than once to avoid hitting her. Isabella was his sort of woman; she had nerve.

He'd had sex with many women but had cared for only two, Karen and Isabella. He'd hunted and trapped many animals but

135

felt an affinity for only one, the dappled leopard which, unlike its cousin the cheetah, couldn't be tamed to trot on a leash beside an exhibitionist human owner, and which preferred the solitude of the tree to the community of the plains.

He was thinking of Isabella's delight on the day he'd given her a present of a gold bangle when there was a ring at the front door.

Two men stood on the doorstep.

'Mr Phelan?'

'Who are you?'

One of the men presented a card. 'I'm Detective Inspector Cook and my colleague is Detective Sergeant Wilkins.'

'What do you want?'

'If we may come in, we'll tell you.'

Phelan gave a long cold look and said, 'All right, come in, I've got something to tell you too.'

He led the way to the sitting room.

'What do you want?'

'What do you want to tell us, Mr Phelan?'

'Lay off. I don't like being watched.'

'Ah, yes . . . May we sit down?'

Phelan made a chopping gesture towards the chairs.

'Would you mind very much, Mr Phelan, if we recorded this conversation? It's for your protection as well as ours.'

'Why should you?'

'We've come in connection with the death of someone called Maxine Eastbank.'

'Who?'

'Maxine Eastbank.'

'Don't know her.'

'That,' said Cook, 'is why it's vital for your interests that we tape all this. As someone who didn't know Miss Eastbank it will save you a lot of time and trouble if we have a verbatim record of the fact.'

While he was speaking Wilkins had unfastened a black briefcase and placed a tape recorder on the glass-topped table where an empty bottle of Chivas Regal stood.

'I've found,' said Cook, 'that people who have nothing to hide have no objection to being taped.'

'Why should I have anything to hide?'

'No reason, but we are obliged to follow up enquiries in a case such as this.'

Phelan saw Wilkins press a button. It was on the tip of his tongue to say he hadn't given permission but he decided to allow them to go ahead. If he couldn't cope with these pallid deadbeats he wasn't the man he thought he was. He said, 'Get on with it. Say what you want to say.'

'You didn't know Maxine Eastbank?'

'Who's she?'

'Her body was found in a copse on the edge of Epping Forest.'

Phelan made a show of recollection. 'I think I've read about it in your papers.'

'It was in the papers,' Cook agreed, 'but we have reason to believe you knew this lady.'

'Reason?' What reason?'

Very slowly, as if the movement was made with the utmost reluctance, Cook reached into his pocket and produced a small red leather book.

'This contains a list of Miss Eastbank's clients. Your name is among them.'

Phelan was taken aback. 'Clients?'

'A euphemism, Mr Phelan. She was a prostitute.'

'I know, but what makes you think I was a client?'

'You know she was a prostitute?'

'I read about it.'

'Read about it in our papers?'

'That's right.'

'Which papers?'

'I don't know. Newspapers.'

'Do you take a regular newspaper?'

'Look, I don't have to put up with this. Get to the point.'

'Very well,' said Cook. 'Where were you on the twenty-seventh and twenty-eighth September?'

'I don't know.'

'A pity. It would be most helpful if you could remember.'

A silence expanded between the two men. It filled the room and seeped through open french windows into the small garden outside. Phelan who knew the language of silences recognised this as the silence of the forest when small creatures knew a predator was abroad and survival depended on staying motion-less.

He remained silent, motionless, not that he was small but he sensed that predators were abroad.

Cook took a different tack. 'You, or someone resembling

137

you, has been identified as a man who was near the place where Miss Eastbank's body was found. That's why I'd like to know where you were on the dates I've mentioned.'

'Near the place . . . Who says so?'

'A man who gave you, or someone very like you, a lift in his car to Epping.'

'If he thinks it was me, he's mistaken.'

'He may be, but he's seen a photograph of you and thinks you're the person he picked up, but he says if he could hear your voice he'd be absolutely certain.'

Phelan looked at the tape recorder and just managed to prevent himself from reaching out to switch it off.

But Cook had noticed the suppressed involuntary movement. 'Yes,' he said, 'we've got a record of your voice on that tape. We also have your name in an address book. So, if you weren't the man who was on the fringe of Epping Forest very late on the twenty-eighth or early on the twenty-ninth September, and you never flagged down a mini-cab driver, please let me know where you were and we won't detain you any more.'

'To hell with that,' said Phelan. 'I don't have to account to you.'

'No?' Cook leaned forward and peered at Phelan's left wrist. 'That's a nice watch. How long have you had it?'

'This?' Phelan looked down at the watch he'd purchased that morning. 'I've had it years.'

'Hours, Mr Phelan, not years. I'm sure that must have been a slip of the tongue. Hours, yes?'

'What's it to you?' Attack was usually the best method of defence, and one should never explain, never apologise. 'I'm not accountable to you. If you've come to charge me with something, get on with it. Otherwise, get out.'

Cook reached into his pocket and pulled out a watch. 'Is this yours?'

Phelan peered at a Rolex oyster fastened to the strap he'd bought from an Arab trader in Mombasa. 'Why should it be mine?' he asked.

'You haven't lost such a watch recently?'

'No.'

'So you're not making any claim to this one?'

'That's right.'

'It was found by Miss Eastbank's body early in the morning on the twenty-ninth September. I have reason to believe it is yours.'

'What reason?'

Cook pointed to the watch on Phelan's wrist. 'You purchased that this morning from a market stall.'

'So what if I did?'

'To replace this one.' Cook held up the Rolex.

'It was to replace a watch. My old one went *kaput*. I slung it.'

'You threw away a watch?' Cook sounded surprised. 'It must have been old and worthless.'

'It was. I'd had it years.'

'What was its make?' Cook fired the question like a bullet. It hit its target. Phelan tried to think of a make of watch that wasn't a Rolex.

'You had it years and you can't remember the make,' Cook pressed.

Phelan glanced at the watch he'd bought earlier. 'It was the same as this. A Timex.'

'You could prove that, if necessary?'

'Why should it be necessary?'

'It won't be necessary if you can give me a satisfactory explanation of where you were throughout the twenty-seventh and twenty-eighth of last month.'

'I can't say. I don't keep a diary.'

A momentary weariness crossed Cook's face. It was the weariness of someone who hasn't slept properly for many nights and must now summon the mental energy to explain to a stubbornly obstructive man the reason why his movements on specified dates had to be accounted for.

'On the evening of the twenty-sixth,' Cook began, 'you were a guest on a television show. On the morning of the twenty-ninth you turned up at your hotel looking dishevelled and unshaven after not having been at the hotel, for sleeping at any rate, from when the maid made up your bed on the morning of the twenty-sixth. So you slept, or stayed, elsewhere on the nights of the twenty-sixth, the twenty-seventh and twenty-eighth. You were last seen at around eight ten p.m. on the twenty-sixth in the company of an attractive young lady. Miss Eastbank was murdered at some time on the night of the twenty-eighth. Your name is in a book containing names of her clients. Just try, if you will, to remember where you were on the dates in question.'

The forest-like silence which followed became oppressive. The predator was moving in for the kill.

'I'm waiting, Mr Phelan.'

'I don't remember.'

'Then I must tell you something else. We dusted a number of articles and furnishings in Miss Eastbank's house and came up with a great number of fingerprints. Some of these have been cleared. Quite a few men have already assisted in our enquiries and all gave permission for their fingerprints to be taken. I assume you'll have no objection to yours being taken. Am I right?'

Phelan tried to recollect where he might have left prints. They would certainly be on the bars of the cage where he did isometric exercises, on the whisky bottle, possibly also on the Elsan. If any of these had been dusted and his fingerprints tallied then it would prove he had been in the house and it would be presumed he'd been a so-called client.

'Am I right, Mr Phelan?' Cook repeated.

If he did give fingerprints, and they did tally, it would not only be presumed that he had been a client but also that he had a motive for murder. Any poor devil who had been driven beyond the limits of pleasurable endurance would want to kill. And the fact that the Eastbank bitch had included his name in her book of clients would clinch matters.

'Am I right?' Cook persisted.

How the hell could he explain the missing two days? Cindy, if she hadn't deserted him, might have been willing to provide an alibi.

'I think I must ask you to come with us, Mr Phelan. Your answers have been quite unsatisfactory. We shall need to have your fingerprints and we shall need a signed statement from you as to your whereabouts on the relevant dates, details of your old watch, where you "slung" it, and we shall need to bring along a witness who gave someone like you a lift in his car late on the night of the twenty-eighth.'

Cook stood up but Phelan remained seated. Wilkins began to stand and then remained for a moment half-poised over his chair before completing the upright movement.

'Are you arresting me?'

'No, I'm taking you in for questioning. If you are innocent I can't see what possible objection you can have. It'll clear you once and for all.'

Phelan knew he was cornered and the predator was inescapable. From now on it was a matter of playing for time and hoping Samson would come up with evidence to exonerate him.

He stood up. 'I'd like to make a phone call first.'

'By all means,' said Cook.

'It's a private call.'

'Fair enough. We'll wait outside.' Cook turned to his deputy. 'Brian, you go out and wait in that back-yard, will you? I'll wait in the hallway.'

As they moved in different directions Phelan realised they were giving him no chance of escape. When he was alone he dialled Samson's number. The call was answered by Shandy.

'This is Paul Phelan. Is your boss back yet?'

'Not yet, Mr Phelan.'

'Will you give him a message. Tell him I've got the police here and they're taking me away for questioning. It looks as if I might be on a murder charge. Tell him to come up with something quick. OK?'

'Where are they taking you?'

'Hold on.' Phelan hurried to the door. 'Where are we going?' he asked Cook who was in the hallway gazing at framed prints of eighteenth-century cartoons.

'We'll go to the police station at Northwick Green.'

Phelan hurried back to the phone. 'Northwick Green police station. Tell him it's urgent that he comes up with something good.'

'I will. Good luck.'

'I need it. Goodbye.'

Phelan put down the phone. It was then he noticed the tape recorder was still running. Everything had been recorded. The police hadn't been giving anything away when they had allowed him privacy. He took a deep breath and went to face his newest enemy.

'Are we likely to be long?' he asked Cook.

'That will depend on you and how far you're prepared to co-operate, and on the outcome of our further enquiries.'

'What further enquiries?'

'We are just beginning, Mr Phelan. We need to examine in greater detail what you've already said and probably ask a few more questions, depending on your replies.'

Phelan always travelled light and so long as he had passport, money, shaving tackle and a toothbrush, he could go anywhere. He decided to dispense with the shaving tackle.

'I'll just get my jacket,' he said, and he went into a small lobby.

After checking that the minimum essentials were in the pockets he slipped on the jacket and rejoined Cook. 'Let's go,' he said.

CHAPTER 18

Although in his earlier years as an enquiry agent debt-collecting had been Samson's most disliked chore he had learned the skills of obtaining both illegal and permitted entries to people's homes. As his business became more prosperous he used techniques learned earlier to good advantage. Most householders were unwilling to admit strangers to their homes without some evidence that their call was on official business. Samson usually stated that he was calling as a private detective or an enquiry agent and then implied that the visit was in a semi-official capacity.

One of his most successful ploys was to exploit greed. It was simple, through records at Somerset House, to discover the names of parents of the man he wished to question. He would note the mother's maiden name which, for example, might be Henderson, go to the man's house, state that he was an enquiry agent who was acting for representatives of a millionaire called James Henderson who had recently died intestate in Tasmania. A search was being made for any distant relatives . . . 'Although there are any number of Hendersons in the country my researches lead me to believe that you, through your mother, might be entitled to share in the estate. May I come in and discuss the matter?' If the man asked why, of all the Hendersons, he should have been singled out Samson would say there was a piece of further information which narrowed the field but he wasn't at liberty to disclose it. After having been invited inside, and discovering what he'd come to find out, he'd promise to get in touch again if there was good news. There never was.

On his way to Streatham in a hired car he ran through the various methods of gaining entry to the house occupied by the woman who signed herself 'Pam'. Without knowing her surname the inheritance ploy wouldn't work, and if she was a woman living on her own she would be cautious of admitting him unless he had a convincing reason for his call. Moreover, there was a chance she might not be at home and then, unless he could find out from a neighbour when she was due to return, he would have had a wasted journey.

If she opened the door to him he would honestly state his name and occupation. Masquerading as a meter reader or a purchaser of any old silver was for novices and crooks who specialised in thieving from lonely old ladies. The problem was how to impress a woman called Pam with a plausible cover story. He knew nothing of Pam except that she was on the extreme fringe of the animal rights movement and was probably about the same age as Maxine Eastbank. In her letter she had written, 'To hell with men', and this might suggest a lesbian relationship existed between the two women but it was a naive assumption made by far too many men that women who had close relationships, and shared an antipathy towards men, must automatically be lesbians. Samson had never made this mistake.

From the sketchy outline of Pam he had to create an opening so compelling that she would feel obliged to invite him into her home. He was still deep in thought when the car turned off the main road to the south coast and entered a residential area of identical semi-detached houses built in the 1930s.

The uniformity of the houses under a uniform blanket of grey cloud gave the area that strangely lifeless look which occurs when most suburban homes have been drained of humanity by mass commuting into central London, and the only people to be seen in the streets are either women with children under school age or old people who have never managed to break away from the crushing anonymity of the locality.

As the car turned into another road identical to the last Samson told the driver to stop. 'Stay here or hereabouts,' he said. 'I don't know how long I'll be.'

He walked down the road until he came to number 43. After pausing to look at the house's exterior, and noting that all windows were backed by net curtains, he walked up a narrow concrete path to the front door. He pressed the doorbell. This was the critical moment. Would there be a response?

He waited. An aircraft on its way to Heathrow passed overhead. Then he heard the sound of footsteps and a click as a catch slid back.

A woman aged about thirty with short spiky ginger hair and wearing a baggy grey sweater and faded blue jeans stood in the doorway. She had a small, pale face with brown eyes which looked warily at him. She waited for him to speak.

'My name is John Samson. I am a private enquiry agent and I need as a matter of great urgency to speak with someone known as Pam.' As he was speaking he noticed that she was wearing rings on all the fingers of her left hand; he felt sure that not only had he come to the right place but he had found the right woman. 'It won't take long,' he said.

'Why do you want to speak to her?'

She had an accent which Samson associated with Bromley rather than Streatham.

'May I come in?' he asked politely. 'It's not something to discuss outside. It is a very private matter.'

She looked intently at him. He gazed benignly back at her. 'I need to know a bit more before I let you in,' she said.

'Very well. I'm employed by a top firm of lawyers to find their client, a Mr Paul Phelan. He has disappeared and they have reason to fear for his safety.'

At the mention of Phelan's name a fleeting expression of anxiety crossed her face. 'I don't see how I can help,' she said, 'I've never heard of him.'

Samson shook his head sadly. 'Not true, I'm afraid. You were with him in the basement of a house in Stamford Hill in the company of someone called Maxine Eastbank. This was only a few days ago. I do have to speak to you urgently, Pam. . . . May I call you "Pam"?'

Her beringed hand went to her mouth. 'Oh, my God,' she said.

'May I come in? It is very important. I don't really want to go to the police to reveal what I know. If you can help me that may not be necessary.'

She stepped back. 'All right.'

She led the way to a front room where chairs stood all round the perimeter and, in the centre, a table was covered with pamphlets and magazines about animals. Animal rights posters hung on the walls. Except for the absence of sick pets the place might have been a veterinary surgeon's waiting room.

Samson sat down and partly opened a briefcase similar to that used by Wilkins. He took out a sheaf of papers, placed them

145

beside him, and switched on a tape recorder.

'Do you know where Mr Phelan is?' he asked.

'I haven't the faintest idea. I really haven't.'

'When did you last see him?'

She drew a breath, began to say something, changed her mind and said, 'Wait a minute. What makes you think I've seen him at all? I knew Maxine, that's true. And her house.'

'And the basement,' Samson chipped in, 'and what was in the basement, and what happened inside a cage when Mr Phelan was naked and defenceless.'

'I'm not responsible for what happened to Maxine's clients. That was her business, not mine, and never has been.'

'Mr Phelan wasn't a client,' said Samson quietly, 'and you know he wasn't a client. He was captured like a wild animal and put through the hoops like a circus animal. Please don't fence with me. I know the score and unless you are level with me I shall go straight to the police.'

She had been standing by the table. Now she sat down, her pale face almost a chalky white. She looked as though she was about to faint.

'It was Maxine's idea to do it. She was very strong-willed. There was something about her. She could make women, as well as men, do things against their will. She sometimes said, and she meant it, that she was a princess of darkness and had supernatural powers.'

'Really? Then I'm surprised she had a crucifix in her bedroom. People with occult tendencies aren't known to like the sign of the cross. The opposite.'

'You know about her bedroom?'

'I know a lot, Pam.'

'The crucifix was typical of her. She reckoned she could make the opposition impotent by treating its symbols like household objects.'

'That may be,' said Samson drily, 'but her fancies and fantasies are no concern of mine. Anyway, she's dead, and I believe you know who killed her.'

She seemed to get a grip on herself and the normal pallor returned to her face.

'I don't know, but I can guess,' she said.

'What's your guess?' Samson asked.

'Him. Phelan. He killed her and that's why he's missing now.'

Samson shook his head. 'Not so. I have evidence that he couldn't possibly have killed her.'

'What evidence?'

She was calling his bluff and he had a choice of replies. He could say he wasn't willing to disclose the source of his evidence, he could threaten to take details of the unspecified evidence to the police, or he could take a chance that she, possibly aided by someone called Cynth, had taken Phelan to Epping Forest and dumped him on its borders. If they had, were they accompanied by Maxine Eastbank? He decided to take the chance.

'How did you get to Epping Forest?' he asked. 'By car? By van?'

'What makes you think I was there?'

'You were. And who was the other one? Cynth? Cynthia? You must be fairly strong women to have shifted all that dead weight.'

She paled again and almost inaudibly she asked, 'What do you mean – all that dead weight?'

Samson realised there was more to the question than a simple enquiry. He was about to say, 'The weight of Mr Phelan's unconscious body' but changed it to, 'I'm talking of body weight.'

'I don't know what you mean.'

'Let's start again,' said Samson patiently. 'I will admit I don't know which of you is expert in administering drugs, but one of you is. If I had to hazard a guess, I'd say it was Cynth.'

She was sitting on the edge of her seat, every muscle tensed, straining forward as if the battle between her and Samson was of all-consuming intensity which she must win at all costs.

'I don't know how the hell you know about Cynth and me, but you're not getting anything out of me.'

'I have already. It's only a matter of tying up some loose ends. One of you has a knowledge of, and access to, drugs. But we'll leave that for the moment. When you or she injected Mr Phelan with a drug after he'd managed to get Maxine off balance in the cage, how did Maxine react?'

She stood up. 'That's enough. I don't want to talk about it any more.'

'Talk about what?'

She walked to the door. 'Goodbye.'

147

Samson didn't move. 'You don't strike me as the sort of woman to condone torture,' he said. 'But I expect you thought it was all in a good cause.'

'Will you go or shall I call the police?'

Samson, at his most avuncular, said, 'Call the police, my dear. I've got a lot to tell them.'

She stood by the door, uncertain what to do next. He sat immobile, but although he looked like a beached whale, he was trying to fathom why she'd been thrown when he'd said it needed strength to shift so much dead weight.

'It's nothing to do with me,' she said.

'It's everything to do with you. Maxine Eastbank has been killed and now Mr Phelan may have been disposed of.'

'He was all right.'

Samson repeated her words. 'He was all right? You mean he was all right when you left him?'

'Please go.'

'I expect you want to give Cynth a call to warn her there's a nosy private eye on her trail.'

She remained by the door like someone in no-man's-land who doesn't know how to reach safe territory, stranded and indecisive. Samson remained firmly on his chair as though welded to it. Why had she been thrown by 'dead weight'? Was it the 'dead' or the 'weight' which had disturbed her?

'Please go,' she said. 'I'm not saying any more.'

'What are you afraid of?' he asked.

She gripped the door handle as though she needed solid support.

'I don't know how you found me, and I don't know where he is. I haven't got anything more to say.'

'But you don't deny you were there when Maxine cracked a whip at him and tried to make him perform for her.'

In a whisper she said, 'No, I don't deny it. But it was her idea, not mine.'

'Even though you and Cynth mounted "Operation White Tigers"?'

'How did you know about that?'

'As I've told you, I know a lot.'

'She made us do it.'

'Made,' said Samson scornfully, 'no one can make someone else do something they don't want to do.'

148

'They can if they've got something on you.'

'And what had she got on you?'

'I'm not saying.'

'Drugs? Lethal drugs, addictive drugs, tranquillising drugs?'

'No.'

'Who stuck the needle in?'

She didn't reply.

'We don't seem to be getting very far,' said Samson equably, 'so I'll try a different approach. I've told you one small lie, but only one.'

She was gripping the door handle so tightly that her knuckles were a white ridge. 'What lie?'

'I'm not employed by lawyers.'

He watched the information sink in and take root. Her brown eyes and small face were wonderfully expressive. A carousel of emotions spun around her features; there was uncertainty, apprehension, anger, and finally, fear.

'Why are you here then?'

'I'm employed by Mr Phelan who has retained me to find you. He wants revenge. I think he's wrong. I think there should be a legal prosecution by the police on a criminal charge. But he wants to deal with you himself. I wouldn't like to be answerable for the consequences, if he does.'

'You know where he is? He's not missing?'

'He's disappeared from the public eye but, yes, I know where he is, and heaven help you if I tell him where you are.'

'I didn't have anything to do with it. It was all Maxine's idea.'

'Since she's dead,' said Samson flatly, 'she can't confirm or deny that. But who killed her? That's what I want to know. Mr Phelan doesn't seem so interested in that detail. So far as he's concerned, it's one down and two to go. He wants me to find you and your friend, Cynth, and then he'll take the law into his own hands. But I'm willing to do a deal with you.'

'A deal?' Hope appeared in her eyes.

'Come and sit down. You're letting in a draught.'

She closed the door and obediently went to the chair she'd vacated. 'What deal?' she asked.

'You tell me exactly what happened after Mr Phelan was knocked out and I'll do my best to see he doesn't harm you.'

'How can I be sure?' she asked. 'You've told one lie, that could be a lie too.'

It was then that Samson made the connection which had been puzzling him, her blanched face and the words 'dead weight'.

'Just tell me one thing,' he said. 'How did you get Mr Phelan from your transport to the place where he found himself when he recovered consciousness?'

Her head drooped and she spoke so quietly he had to ask her to repeat what she had said.

'We carried him. Cynth took the top half. I held his legs.'

If they had carried him, the stripes on Phelan's back hadn't been caused through being dragged along the ground. So what had caused the injury?

'Did Maxine flog him while he was unconscious?' he asked.

Her hand went to her mouth and she began to sob. 'It was terrible. We couldn't stand it.'

'What did she do?'

'She went wild. It was terrifying. We had to stick him up against the wall. His wrists were fastened to the wall and she started using the whip on his bare back. She was screaming at him, telling him she'd give him a lesson he'd never forget. But he couldn't hear her. He was out to the wide. I couldn't stand it. I shouted at her to stop. She didn't. She was mad. She'd have flogged him to death. I tried to grab the whip from her. We struggled and then, when it looked as if she was going to get the better of me, Cynth grabbed a cane off the wall and hit her on the head with the knobbed end.'

The confession left her sobbing and breathless. Samson gave her a few moments to recover and then said, 'So it wasn't one body you carried, but two. Both dead weight.'

'I never thought it would end like that.'

'I don't suppose you did. But your intervention may have saved his life even if it cost hers.' Samson paused. 'Why did you leave his watch beside her body? Was it to incriminate him?'

She looked askance. 'His watch?'

'His wrist-watch was found beside her body.'

'I don't know about that. We just dumped them and then dumped his clothes beside him. Maybe the watch fell out of his clothes. When we stripped him we took it off and put it in his jacket pocket. It must have fallen out.'

'Did you leave Mr Phelan and Maxine close to each other?'

'Fairly close. She was by a bush and he was about a couple of yards away.'

150

'I don't think he saw her.'

'Maybe not. It was dark and not much of a moon.' Her voice became agonised. 'What are you going to do?'

'Does Cynth live here with you?'

'Yes.'

'When is she due back?'

'This evening.'

'What's her job?'

'She's a research scientist.'

'Working for a pharmaceutical company?'

'Yes.'

'Has access to drugs?'

'Yes . . . What are you going to do?'

'Right now,' said Samson, 'I'm going back to my office. I shall then tell my client what happened and that earns my fee. I shall then advise him to get out of the country fast.'

'Will he go?'

Samson smiled. 'I think he will.'

'What about us? Cynth and me? We've been on hot bricks. It's a murder although it wasn't meant, and the police are on to it. When you said who you were I thought for an awful moment you were from the police.'

Samson stood up. 'That's the worst thing that's been said to me for a long time.'

'I didn't mean it.' Her range of facial expressions was in disarray. Sincerity was followed by an uncertain smile which was followed by the pleading look of a mute beggar. 'You won't tell him where we are, will you?'

'I'm not making any promises but it's not my intention to send him here. As for what you did, it sounds to me more like manslaughter than murder, but that's a matter for the police if ever they catch up with you. One more thing. Your surname, please?'

'Stephens.'

'And Cynth's surname?'

'It's the same. We're sisters.'

'I see. And Maxine was equally fond of you both?'

She lowered her eyes. 'Yes.'

Samson replaced the sheaf of papers in his briefcase and snapped it shut. 'Goodbye, Miss Stephens. I recommend more peaceful forms of protest in future, but that's up to you.'

Before returning to his office Samson called on a firm he was advising on security precautions. When he finally appeared Shandy greeted him with, 'Thank heavens you're back.'

'Don't tell me you've seen another mouse. We shall have to get a cat.'

'It's no time for joking. The police have got Phelan. He thinks he's going to be on a murder charge.'

'Where is he?'

'Northwick Green police station.'

'It's all go,' said Samson wearily. 'Anything else to report?'

'No. What are you going to do?'

'Go to Northwick Green with this.' He tapped his briefcase. 'It contains a confession to the homicide of Maxine Eastbank. I'll fill you in on the details later.'

CHAPTER 19

A police car was waiting for Cook. Phelan recognised the driver as the man with dead eyes. 'I might have guessed you'd be around,' he said. 'Haven't you got a home to go to?'

Cook opened the back door. 'After you, Mr Phelan.'

Wilkins sat in front with the driver.

The car moved smoothly away and soon joined the flow of traffic travelling past the south side of Hyde Park.

No one spoke.

Phelan looked out of the window as if taking an interest in street scenes but his thoughts were concentrated on how to avoid further interrogation with the probability of arrest on a charge of murder and a remand in custody. Even if he obtained bail, and Cook would surely oppose bail, his passport would be taken away.

The car came to a halt at a pedestrian crossing and three youths sauntered across. Phelan looked at the door handle. If he tried to escape at a pedestrian crossing, or when the car stopped at traffic lights, it was almost certain Cook could grab him before he got out.

The car moved forward again.

He might be able temporarily to immobilise Cook, but how? A chop to the throat might be difficult to aim but a head butt might work. Murunga, who had been in many fights, had taught him the art of head-butting, but here again it would be difficult to get the right angle even if he could get the force.

The car was now entering unfamiliar territory as it weaved in and out of heavy traffic. At last he spoke. 'How much further?'

'About another ten minutes,' said Cook.

Ten minutes, and he still hadn't planned the means of escape. Once inside the police station it would be more difficult. He could ask to go to the toilet but might find its windows barred.

All he could hope for was an opportunity, however slight, and to seize it when it appeared.

The car entered a quieter road where other cars were parked on both sides of the street. Wilkins turned to the driver and said something about double yellow lines, and the driver replied, 'I'd clobber the lot.'

The car slowed by a modern red-brick building which had a blue lamp outside. They had arrived. The car turned into a wide passageway beside the building and came to a halt near a row of police cars in a yard at the rear.

'We're here,' said Cook and he reached for his door handle. Phelan did the same. When he saw Cook beginning to step out he moved fast and the moment his feet touched the ground he began running. A voice shouted, 'Stop him!'

A uniformed policeman appeared ahead of Phelan, his arms spread wide. Phelan didn't pause, he swerved to the left and then at the last moment swerved to the right. The policeman wasn't off balance; he lunged to his left and caught hold of Phelan's jacket. For a split-second both men faced each other and then Phelan lashed out with his fist, hit the policeman squarely on the face, and twisted himself free as blood began pouring from the other man's nose.

If they couldn't charge him before, they'd certainly charge him now. Phelan sprinted down the street which was filled with parked cars. He could hear shouting behind him, and then the siren of a police car.

A few yards ahead a car with a grey-haired man at the wheel was pulling out from a parking space. It was pointing in the direction of the police station. Phelan raced across the road, wrenched open the rear door, jumped inside and gripped the nape of the driver's neck. 'Keep going,' he said, 'or you're dead.'

The driver gasped and jabbed at the accelerator. Phelan glimpsed the police car swerving to miss a head-on collision. A sharp screech of metallic injury as the sides of the cars scraped and Phelan's car was clear. 'Faster,' he hissed as they passed the police station and he caught sight of Cook and two other men.

'Where?' said the driver in an agonised voice as they reached a T-junction.

'Left.'

The car swerved to the left and almost hit a cyclist as Phelan increased pressure on the driver's neck.

'Do you know this area?' he asked.

'Yes.'

'Get me to the nearest Tube station and I'll bid you goodbye.'

'I will. It's not far. But for God's sake, let go. You're too close to the carotid artery. I shall black out.'

Phelan relaxed his grip. 'You a medic?' he asked.

'I am, and I'm on call. I've got a patient with a serious cardiac condition waiting for me.'

'He'll have to wait a bit longer.'

After a minute's silence the driver said, 'There it is. Ahead on the right.'

'Good. Pull in opposite.'

'What about the damage to my car?'

'Charge it to your insurance company or the police.'

The driver slowed down. 'What do they want you for?' he asked.

'Murder,' replied Phelan, 'so thank your lucky stars you obliged.'

As the car came to a halt he jumped out and without another word ran across the road and into the underground station.

Samson said, 'Wait here or hereabouts,' to the chauffeur of his hired car. He alighted, briefcase in hand, and walked to the entrance of Northwick Green police station.

'I'd like to see Detective Inspector Cook,' he said to the desk sergeant.

'What name, sir?'

'Samson. John Samson.'

The sergeant gave him a curious look. 'I think he'll be glad to see you, sir.'

Keeping his eyes fixed on Samson he picked up a phone. 'Mr John Samson to see you, sir.' The flicker of a smile passed across his face before he replaced the phone. 'Please come with me,' he said to Samson.

Cook didn't stand up when Samson entered. From his desk he waved his hand at a chair. 'Take a seat.'

Samson sat down.

Cook picked up his pencil and began twirling it. 'Where is your client?' he asked.

'My client? I have more than one client. Which client do you mean?'

The pencil moved so fast it was almost a blur. 'You know which client. Phelan.'

'Isn't he with you?'

'He is not.'

'My secretary had a message that you were bringing him here for more questioning.'

'We did, but he left before we could ask any questions. So I repeat, where is your client?'

'You mean, he gave you the slip?'

'If you care to put it like that. I hope I don't have to remind you of the penalties for being an accessory.'

'How could I be an accessory to something I didn't know anything about?'

'Mr Samson,' said Cook slowly, making the name seem to have more than two syllables, 'you know a murder has been committed. I'm speaking of being an accessory after that fact.'

'That fact?' Samson smiled. 'I'm still not sure what fact you mean. I haven't aided or abetted my client. The reverse. But if you can prove otherwise, go ahead. As a subscriber to police charities I don't like seeing police funds wasted, but if you think you have something you can pin on me, go ahead.'

The pencil stopped twirling. Cook put it down and reached for a phone. 'Ask Sergeant Wilkins to come in, please.' To Samson he said, 'I think we need a witness.'

'Witness to what?'

'Your attempts to influence me by referring to your donations to police charities.' He paused. 'Among other things,' he added.

'Heaven forbid,' said Samson. 'Our police force is the best in the world. I've often heard it said.'

A light knock on the door and Wilkins entered.

'Ah, Brian, take a seat. Any news of the fugitive?'

'Not yet, sir.'

'All airports and seaports have been alerted?'

'They have.'

'He won't get far.' Cook turned his attention to Samson. 'Now then, I've heard you're a Time buff, and I've seen your collection of clocks, but the only time I'm concerned with is time, meaning a life sentence, for the killer of Maxine Eastbank.'

'Quite right too,' said Samson.

'You're here for the same purpose, I hope.'

'As I've told you, I came here to see my client, but evidently he gave you the slip. How did he manage that?'

'That's my business, not yours. But I'll tell you this. He assaulted a policeman who was acting in the execution of his duty and we'll get him for that too.'

'Assault? I am sorry to hear that,' said Samson solicitously. 'I hope your man wasn't hurt, but maybe I can bring you a little cheer.'

'Oh, yes? How?'

Samson opened his briefcase and took out a tape. He held it up. 'This is a record of a conversation I had this afternoon with someone who was present when Miss Eastbank was killed.'

Cook picked up the pencil lying on his desk, gave it a few twirls between his fingers and put it down.

'I should like to hear it,' he said.

'You shall, but first I must fill you in with some background.'

Cook listened intently as Samson described Phelan's ordeal. When the account was finished, he said, 'I've had any number of punters with way-out reasons for having visited Eastbank, but that beats the lot. So, what's on that tape?'

Samson inserted the tape and pressed a switch.

When the tape had finished Cook said, 'What's this woman's address?'

Samson told him.

Cook turned to Wilkins. 'Bring her in,' he said tersely.

'Right.' Wilkins left the room.

'I shall have to ask you to wait. I shall need verification of the tape, and I'd like you to be present.'

Samson's eyelids drooped; it looked as if he was about to fall asleep. 'Is that really necessary?' he asked. 'She's bound to verify it. If she doesn't the voiceprints will match.'

'Nevertheless I'd like you both present. In the meanwhile' – Cook stood up – 'I'll take you to a room we use as a waiting room when required. I trust you'll stay.'

'I shall stay,' said Samson. 'My client's interests demand it.'

'May I have the tape, please?'

Samson handed it over.

'Thank you. Now come with me, please.'

When, after an hour's wait, Samson was recalled to Cook's room he found Wilkins with another plain-clothes policeman, and Pam Stephens, already there.

She greeted him with, 'You stinking rotten sod.'

157

Samson bowed politely. 'Your servant, ma'am.'

'You . . . you . . .' She was inarticulate with anger. 'You filthy creep,' she managed at last.

'Now, now, that's enough,' said Cook, not sharply but in a conciliatory tone as if reluctant to stop the abuse. 'I want you to listen to this, Miss Stephens,' he went on, 'and tell me whether this is your voice.'

The tape began to run. The sound of a woman sobbing was followed by, 'It was terrible. We couldn't stand it. . . . She went wild. It was terrifying. We had to stick him up against the wall . . .'

'Stop it,' screamed Pam Stephens. 'Stop it!'

Cook reached out and stopped the tape. 'Your voice?' he asked.

'Yes, yes. Of course it is.'

Cook turned to Samson. 'I'll keep the tape for the time being, if you don't mind.'

Samson shrugged. 'I don't need it. And now, if I'm not needed either, I'd like to get back to my office. But I have one request to make.'

'Yes?'

'Should you apprehend my client I should like to be informed at once.'

Cook thought for a moment before giving the vestige of a smile. 'I don't see why not. After all, rather late in the day, you have given some co-operation.'

'Yes,' said Samson. 'I have been of some service to the State.'

Very late that evening, after Cynthia Stephens had been arrested and charged with murder, and Cook was preparing to go home he turned to Wilkins and said, 'Fat he may be, but he's not quite the slob I thought he was.'

Wilkins smothered a yawn.

'You're sleepy, Brian,' Cook observed. 'Well, so am I. And I think tonight I'll sleep well.'

CHAPTER 20

The trial was widely reported. To the chagrin of the animal rights group involved there was hardly any mention of the reason for the capture of the detested trapper of rare wild animals and negligible publicity for their cause. Most newspaper reportage emphasised the bizarre background to the case as this gave scope for readership titillation.

Cynthia Stephens pleaded not guilty to the charge of murder but guilty to the lesser charge of manslaughter. Her plea was accepted by the prosecution.

After paying tribute to Detective Inspector Cook for his painstaking conduct of the investigation (details of which were not fully revealed) the trial judge sentenced Cynthia Stephens to two years' imprisonment. Her sister, Pam, was given a similar sentence but it was suspended.

Although Phelan's name was mentioned a number of times, and this gave him newsworthy notoriety, nobody knew where he was or how to find him. He had disappeared completely. The fact that he had escaped from the precincts of Northwick Green police station, and had assaulted a policeman who had tried to restrain him, was not mentioned in court.

Like a safety match the sensational story flamed briefly and died and soon had as much news value as a dead matchstick. The death of a man-tamer was relegated to the mausoleum of pulp magazine true life stories and arcane criminological studies. Cook moved on to other cases, and only Samson periodically wondered what had happened to his client.

One day, when he had given up hope of hearing anything, a letter arrived postmarked Nairobi. It contained a banker's draft for one hundred pounds and a letter from Phelan.

Dear Mr Samson,

I read about the trial in an overseas edition of *The Times*. I am glad that justice of a sort has been done. If what the Stephens sisters said was true, and they did stop me from being flogged to death, I guess I owe them a vote of thanks.

Needless to say, I have kept a low profile since the trial as I don't want to be pestered by the press or cranks. This letter is being posted from Nairobi by a friend. I am in a different country taking a long holiday, the first for years.

There's no harm now in telling you that I was able to fly out of your country in a private aircraft owned by a customer of mine. No names, no pack drill. We landed at le Touquet and from there I made my way to Paris and points south.

I always pay my debts and so am enclosing a draft for a hundred pounds hoping that this meets your charges. It should do. From the reports of the trial it looks as if all the hard work was done by a man called Cook. He is the guy who should get the money. The hundred herewith should more than meet what I owe you.

I have sent a letter to Mr and Mrs Ormerod explaining the situation but giving no address. So do not trouble to contact them.

Best wishes,
P. Phelan

Samson handed the letter to Shandy. 'That's gratitude for you.'

She read it and handed it back. 'You're not in it for gratitude. A hundred pounds is better than nothing.'

'It bugs me he thinks Cook did all the hard work.'

'So what? Who cares what he thinks?'

Thousands of miles away the man they were talking about was lying on a straw mattress gazing at the curved ceiling of a mud hut. On one side was a half-empty whisky bottle and on the other was a woman called Isabella. The hut had no address but Phelan had come home.